SAMPLE THE SEASON'S BEST AND BRIGHTEST

ASIMOV — The native population of a Jovian moon threatens to revolt unless Santa Claus comes to town...

POHL — In a world of consumerism gone mad, the true spirit of Christmas makes an astonishing reappearance...

WOLFE — The toys of a previous year must engage in a brutal and terrifying struggle for survival...

DICKSON — A bizarre alien creature gives the most precious Christmas gift of all: a life...

*Other Anthologies That Will Thrill,
Chill, and Entertain You
from Avon Books*

ARABESQUES and ARABESQUES 2
edited by Susan Shwartz

ARCHITECTURE OF FEAR
edited by Kathryn Cramer and Peter D. Pautz

14 VICIOUS VALENTINES
*edited by Rosalind M. Greenberg,
Martin Harry Greenberg, and Charles G. Waugh*

HAUNTING WOMEN
edited by Alan Ryan

TALES FROM THE SPACEPORT BAR and
ANOTHER ROUND AT THE SPACEPORT BAR
*edited by George H. Scithers and
Darrell Schweitzer*

TROPICAL CHILLS
edited by Tim Sullivan

CHRISTMAS ON GANYMEDE

AND OTHER STORIES

edited by

MARTIN H. GREENBERG

AVON BOOKS ◆ NEW YORK

AVON BOOKS
A division of
The Hearst Corporation
105 Madison Avenue
New York, New York 10016

Acknowledgments

"To Hell With the Stars" by Jack McDevitt. Copyright © 1987 by Davis Publications, Inc. Reprinted by permission of the author.

"A Midwinter's Tale" by Michael Swanwick. Copyright © 1988 by Michael Swanwick. Reprinted by permission of the author and author's agent, Virginia Kidd.

"Christmas on Ganymede" by Isaac Asimov. Copyright © 1941 by Better Publications, Inc.; renewed © 1968 by Isaac Asimov. Reprinted by permission of the author.

"The Falcon and the Falconeer" by Barry N. Malzberg. Copyright © 1969 by Mercury Press, Inc. Reprinted by permission of the author.

"Christmas Roses" by John Christopher. Copyright © 1943 by Street and Smith Publications, Inc.; renewed © 1970 by John Christopher. Reprinted by permission of the Scott Meredith Literary Agency, Inc., 845 Third Avenue, New York, New York 10022.

"Happy Birthday, Dear Jesus" by Frederik Pohl. Copyright © 1956 by Ballantine Books, Inc.; renewed © 1984 by Frederik Pohl. Reprinted by permission of the author.

"The War Beneath the Tree" by Gene Wolfe. Copyright © 1979 by Gene Wolfe. Reprinted by permission of the author and the author's agent, Virginia Kidd.

Contents

viii Contents

To Hell with the Stars

Jack McDevitt

Christmas night.

Will Cutler couldn't get the sentient ocean out of his mind. Or the creature who wanted only to serve man. Or the curious chess game in the portrait that hung in a deserted city on a world halfway across the galaxy. He drew up his knees, propped the book against them, and let his head sink back into the pillows. The sky was dark through the plexidome. It had been snowing most of the evening, but the clouds were beginning to scatter. Orion's belt had appeared, and the lovely double star of Earth and Moon floated among the luminous branches of Granpop's elms. Soft laughter and conversation drifted up the stairs.

The sounds of the party seemed far away, and the *Space Beagle* rode a column of flame down into a silent desert. The glow from the reading lamp was bright on the inside of his eyelids. He broke the beam with

1

his hand, and it dimmed and went out.

The book lay open at his fingertips.

It was hard to believe they were a thousand years old, these stories that were so full of energy and so unlike anything he'd come across before: tales of dark, alien places and gleaming temples under other stars and expeditions to black holes. They don't write like that anymore. Never had, during his lifetime. He'd read some other books from the classical Western period, some Dickens, some Updike, people like that. But these: what was there in the last thousand years to compare with this guy Bradbury?

The night air felt good. It smelled of pine needles and scorched wood and bayberry. And maybe of dinosaurs and rocket fuel.

His father might have been standing at the door for several minutes. "Goodnight, Champ," he whispered, lingering.

"I'm awake, Dad."

He approached the bed. "Lights out already?" he asked. "It's still early." His weight pressed down the mattress.

Will was slow to answer. "I know."

His father adjusted the sheet, pulling it up over the boy's shoulders. "It's supposed to get cold tonight," he said. "Heavy snow by morning." He picked up the book and, without looking at it, placed it atop the night table.

"Dad." The word stopped the subtle shift of weight that would precede the gentle pressure of his father's hand against his shoulder, the final act before withdrawal. "Why didn't we ever go to the stars?"

He was older than most of the other kids' dads.

There had been a time when Will was ashamed of that. He couldn't play ball and he was a lousy hiker. The only time he'd tried to walk out over the Rise, they'd had to get help to bring him home. But he laughed a lot, and he always listened. Will was reaching an age at which he understood how much that counted for. "It costs a lot of money, Will. It's just more than we can manage. You'll be going to Earth in two years to finish school."

The boy stiffened. "Dad, I mean the *stars*. Alpha Centauri, Vega, the Phoenix Nebula—"

"The Phoenix Nebula? I don't think I know that one."

"It's in a story by a man named Clarke. A Jesuit goes there and discovers something terrible—"

The father listened while Will outlined the tale in a few brief sentences. "I don't think," he said, "your mother would approve of your reading such things."

"She gave me the book," he said, smiling softly.

"This one?" It was bound in cassilate, a leather substitute, and its title appeared in silver script: *Great Tales of the Space Age*. He picked it up and looked at it with amusement. The names of the editors appeared on the spine: Asimov and Greenberg. "I don't think we realized, uh, that it was like that. Your mother noticed that it was one of the things they found in the time vault on the Moon a couple of years ago. She thought it would be educational."

"You'd enjoy it, Dad."

His father nodded and glanced at the volume. "What's the Space Age?"

"It's the name that people of the classical period used to refer to their own time. It has to do with the early exploration of the solar system, and the first manned flights. And, I think, the idea that we were going to the stars."

A set of lights moved slowly through the sky. "Oh," his father said. "Well, people have had a lot of strange ideas. History is full of dead gods and formulas to make gold and notions that the world was about to end." He picked up the book, adjusted the lamp, and opened to the contents page. His gray eyes ran down the listings, and a faint smile played about his lips. "The truth of it, Will, is that the stars are a pleasant dream, but no one's ever going out to them."

"Why not?" Will was puzzled at the sound of irritation in his own voice. He was happy to see that his father appeared not to have noticed.

"They're too *far*. They're just too far." He looked up through the plexidome at the splinters of light. "These people, Greenberg and Asimov: they lived, what, a thousand years ago?"

"Twentieth, twenty-first century. Somewhere in there."

"You know that new ship they're using in the outer System? The *Explorer*?"

"Fusion engines," said the boy.

"Yes. Do you know what its top recorded speed is?"

"About a hundred fifty thousand miles an hour."

"Much faster than anything this Greenberg ever saw. Anyhow, if they'd launched an *Explorer* to Alpha Centauri at the time these stories were written, at that speed, do you know how much of the distance they would have covered by now?"

Will had no idea. He would have thought they'd have arrived long ago, but he could see that wasn't going to be the answer. His father produced a minicomp, pushed a few buttons, and smiled. "About five percent. The *Explorer* would need another eighteen-thousand years to get there."

"Long ride," said Will grudgingly.

"You'd want to take a good book."

The boy was silent.

"It's not as if we haven't tried, Will. There's an artificial world, half-built, out beyond Mars someplace. They were going to send out a complete colony, people, farm animals, lakes, forest, everything."

"What happened?"

"It's too *far*. Hell, Will, life is good here. People are happy. There's plenty of real estate in the solar system if folks want to move. In the end, there weren't enough volunteers for the world-ship. I mean, what's the *point*? The people who go would be depriving their kids of any kind of normal life. How would *you* feel about living inside a tube for a lifetime? No beaches. Not real ones anyhow. No sunlight. No new places to explore. And for what? The payoff is so far down the road that, in reality, there *is* no payoff."

"In the stories," Will said, "the ships are very fast."

"I'm sure. But even if you traveled on a light beam, the stars are very far apart. And a ship can't achieve an appreciable fraction of that kind of velocity because it isn't traveling through a vacuum. At, say, a tenth of the speed of light, even a few atoms straying in front of it would blow the damned thing apart."

Outside, the Christmas lights were blue on the snow. "They'd have been disappointed," the boy said, "at how things came out."

"Who would have?"

"Benford. Robinson. Sheffield."

The father looked again at the table of contents. "Oh," he said. He riffled idly through the pages.

"Maybe not. It's hard to tell, of course, with people you don't know. But we've eliminated war, population problems, ecological crises, boundary disputes, racial strife. Everybody eats pretty well now, and for the only time in its history, the human race stands united. I suspect if someone had been able to corner, say—," he paused and flipped some pages, "—Jack Vance, and ask him whether he would have settled for this kind of world, he'd have been delighted. Any sensible man would. He'd have said *to hell with the stars!*"

"No!" The boy's eyes blazed. "He *wouldn't* have been satisfied. None of them would."

"Well, I don't suppose it matters. Physical law is what it is, and it doesn't much matter whether we approve or not. Will, if these ideas hadn't become dated, and absurd, this kind of book wouldn't have disappeared. I mean, we wouldn't even know about *Great Tales of the Space Age* if someone hadn't dropped a copy of the thing into the time capsule. That should tell you something." He got up. "Gotta go, kid. Can't ignore the guests."

A Midwinter's Tale

Michael Swanwick

Maybe I shouldn't tell you about that childhood Christmas Eve in the Stone House, so long ago. My memory is no longer reliable, not since I contracted the brain fever. Soon I'll be strong enough to be reposted offplanet, to some obscure star light years beyond that plangent moon rising over your father's barn, but how much has been burned from my mind! Perhaps none of this actually happened.

Sit on my lap and I'll tell you all. Well then, my knee. No woman was ever ruined by a knee. You laugh, but it's true. Would that it were so easy!

The hell of war as it's now practiced is that its purpose is not so much to gain territory as to deplete the enemy, and thus it's always better to maim than to kill. A corpse can be bagged, burned, and forgotten, but the wounded need special care. Regrowth tanks, false skin, medical personnel, a long convalescent stay

7

on your parents' farm. That's why they will vary their weapons, hit you with obsolete stone axes or toxins or radiation, to force your Command to stock the proper prophylaxes, specialized medicines, obscure skills. Mustard gas is excellent for that purpose, and so was the brain fever.

All those months I lay in the hospital, awash in pain, sometimes hallucinating. Dreaming of ice. When I awoke, weak and not really believing I was alive, parts of my life were gone, randomly burned from my memory. I recall standing at the very top of the iron bridge over the Izveltaya, laughing and throwing my books one by one into the river, while my best friend Fennwolf tried to coax me down. "I'll join the militia! I'll be a soldier!" I shouted hysterically. And so I did. I remember that clearly but just what led up to that preposterous instant is utterly beyond me. Nor can I remember the name of my second-eldest sister, though her face is as plain to me as yours is now. There are odd holes in my memory.

That Christmas Eve is an island of stability in my seachanging memories, as solid in my mind as the Stone House itself, that neolithic cavern in which we led such basic lives that I was never quite sure in which era of history we dwelt. Sometimes the men came in from the hunt, a larl or two pacing ahead content and sleepy-eyed, to lean bloody spears against the walls, and it might be that we lived on Old Earth itself then. Other times, as when they brought in projectors to fill the common room with colored lights, scintillae nesting in the branches of the season's tree, and cool, harmless flames dancing atop the presents, we seemed to belong to a much later age, in some mythologized province of the future.

The house was abustle, the five families all together for this one time of the year, and outlying kin and even a few strangers staying over, so that we had to put bedding in places normally kept closed during the winter, moving furniture into attic lumberrooms, and even at that there were cots and thick bolsters set up in the blind ends of hallways. The women scurried through the passages, scattering uncles here and there, now settling one in an armchair and plumping him up like a cushion, now draping one over a table, cocking up a mustachio for effect. A pleasant time.

Coming back from a visit to the kitchens, where a huge woman I did not know, with flour powdering her big-freckled arms up to the elbows, had shooed me away, I surprised Suki and Georg kissing in the nook behind the great hearth. They had their arms about each other and I stood watching them. Suki was smiling, cheeks red and round. She brushed her hair back with one hand so Georg could nuzzle her ear, turning slightly as she did so, and saw me. She gasped and they broke apart, flushed and startled.

Suki gave me a cookie, dark with molasses and a single stingy, crystalized raisin on top, while Georg sulked. Then she pushed me away, and I heard her laugh as she took Georg's hand to lead him away to some darker forest recess of the house.

Father came in, boots all muddy, to sling a brace of game birds down on the hunt cabinet. He set his unstrung bow and quiver of arrows on their pegs, then hooked an elbow atop the cabinet to accept admiration and a hot drink from mother. The larl padded by, quiet and heavy and content. I followed it around a corner, ancient ambitions of riding the beast rising up within. I could see myself, triumphant before my cousins, high atop the black carnivore. "Flip!" my father called sternly. "Leave Samson alone! He is a bold and noble creature, and I will not have you pestering him."

He had eyes in the back of his head, had my father.

Before I could grow angry, my cousins hurried by, on their way to hoist the straw men into the trees out front, and swept me up along with them. Uncle Chittagong, who looked like a lizard and had to stay in a glass tank for reasons of health, winked at me as I skirled past. From the corner of my eye I saw my second-eldest sister beside him, limned in blue fire.

Forgive me. So little of my childhood remains; vast stretches were lost in the blue icefields I wandered in my illness. My past is like a sunken continent with only mountaintops remaining unsubmerged, a scattered archipelago of events from which to guess the shape of what was lost. Those remaining fragments I treasure all the more, and must pass my hands over them periodically to reassure myself that something remains.

So where was I? Ah, yes: I was in the north bell-tower, my hidey-place in those days, huddled behind Old Blind Pew, the bass of our triad of bells, crying because I had been deemed too young to light one of the yule torches. "Hello!" cried a voice, and then, "Out here, stupid!" I ran to the window, tears forgotten in my astonishment at the sight of my brother Karl silhouetted against the yellowing sky, arms out, treading the roof gables like a tightrope walker.

"You're going to get in trouble for that!" I cried.

"Not if you don't tell!" Knowing full well how I

worshipped him. "Come on down! I've emptied out one of the upper kitchen cupboards. We can crawl in from the pantry. There's a space under the door— we'll see everything!"

Karl turned and his legs tangled under him. He fell. Feet first, he slid down the roof.

I screamed. Karl caught the guttering and swung himself into an open window underneath. His sharp face rematerialized in the gloom, grinning. "Race you to the jade ibis!"

He disappeared, and then I was spinning wildly down the spiral stairs, mad to reach the goal first.

It was not my fault we were caught, for I would never have giggled if Karl hadn't been tickling me to see just how long I could keep silent. I was frightened, but not Karl. He threw his head back and laughed until he cried, even as he was being hauled off by three very angry grandmothers, pleased more by his own roguery than by anything he might have seen.

I myself was led away by an indulgent Katrina, who graphically described the caning I was to receive and then contrived to lose me in the crush of bodies in the common room. I hid behind the goat tapestry until I got bored—not long!—and then Chubkin, Kosmonaut, and Pew rang, and the room emptied.

I tagged along, ignored, among the moving legs, like a marsh bird scuttling through waving grasses. Voices clangoring in the east stairway, we climbed to the highest balcony, to watch the solstice dance. I hooked hands over the crumbling balustrade and pulled myself up on tiptoe so I could look down on the procession as it left the house. For a long time nothing happened, and I remember being annoyed

at how casually the adults were taking all this, standing
about with drinks, not one in ten glancing away from
themselves. Pheidre and Valerian (the younger children had been put to bed, complaining, an hour ago)
began a game of tag, running through the adults, until
they were chastened and ordered with angry shakes
of their arms to be still.

Then the door below opened. The women who
were witches walked solemnly out, clad in hooded
terrycloth robes as if they'd just stepped from the
bath. But they were so silent I was struck with fear.
It seemed as if something cold had reached into the
pink, giggling women I had seen preparing themselves in the kitchen and taken away some warmth or
laughter from them. "Katrina!" I cried in panic, and
she lifted a moon-cold face toward me. Several of the
men exploded in laughter, white steam puffing from
bearded mouths, and one rubbed his knuckles in my
hair. My second-eldest sister drew me away from the
balustrade and hissed at me that I was not to cry out
to the witches, that this was important, that when I
was older I would understand, and in the meantime
if I did not behave myself I would be beaten. To soften
her words, she offered me a sugar crystal, but I turned
away stern and unappeased.

Single-file the women walked out on the rocks to
the east of the house, where all was barren slate swept
free of snow by the wind from the sea, and at a great
distance—you could not make out their faces—
doffed their robes. For a moment they stood motionless in a circle, looking at one another. Then they
began the dance, each wearing nothing but a red ribbon tied about one upper thigh, the long end blowing
free in the breeze.

As they danced their circular dance, the families watched, largely in silence. Sometimes there was a muffled burst of laughter as one of the younger men muttered a racy comment, but mostly they watched with great respect, even a kind of fear. The gusty sky was dark, and flocked with small clouds like purple-headed rams. It was chilly on the roof and I could not imagine how the women withstood it. They danced faster and faster, and the families grew quieter, packing the edges more tightly, until I was forced away from the railing. Cold and bored, I went downstairs, nobody turning to watch me leave, back to the main room, where a fire still smouldered in the hearth.

The room was stuffy when I'd left, and cooler now. I lay down on my stomach before the fireplace. The flagstones smelled of ashes and were gritty to the touch, staining my fingertips as I trailed them in idle little circles. The stones were cold at the edges, slowly growing warmer, and then suddenly too hot and I had to snatch my hand away. The back of the fireplace was black with soot, and I watched the fire-worms crawl over the stone heart-and-hands carved there, as the carbon caught fire and burned out. The log was all embers and would burn for hours.

Something coughed.

I turned and saw something moving in the shadows, an animal. The larl was blacker than black, a hole in the darkness, and my eyes swam to look at him. Slowly, lazily, he strode out onto the stones, stretched his back, yawned a tongue-curling yawn, and then stared at me with those great green eyes.

He spoke.

I was astonished, of course, but not in the way my

father would have been. So much is inexplicable to a child! "Merry Christmas, Flip," the creature said, in a quiet, breathy voice. I could not describe its accent; I have heard nothing quite like it before or since. There was a vast alien amusement in his glance.

"And to you," I said politely.

The larl sat down, curling his body heavily about me. If I had wanted to run, I could not have gotten past him, though that thought did not occur to me then. "There is an ancient legend, Flip, I wonder if you have heard of it, that on Christmas Eve the beasts can speak in human tongue. Have your elders told you that?"

I shook my head.

"They are neglecting you." Such strange humor dwelt in that voice. "There is truth to some of those old legends, if only you knew how to get at it. Though perhaps not all. Some are just stories. Perhaps this is not happening now; perhaps I am not speaking to you at all?"

I shook my head. I did not understand. I said so.

"That is the difference between your kind and mine. My kind understands everything about yours, and yours knows next to nothing about mine. I would like to tell you a story, little one. Would you like that?"

"Yes," I said, for I was young and I liked stories very much.

He began:
When the great ships landed—
Oh God. When—no, no, no, wait. Excuse me. I'm shaken. I just this instant had a vision. It seemed to me that it was night and I was standing at the gates of a cemetery. And suddenly the air was full of light,

planes and cones of light that burst from the ground
and nested twittering in the trees. Fracturing the sky.
I wanted to dance for joy. But the ground crumbled
underfoot and when I looked down the shadow of
the gates touched my toes, a cold rectangle of pro-
foundest black, deep as all eternity, and I was dizzy
and about to fall and I, and I . . .

Enough! I have had this vision before, many times.
It must have been something that impressed me
strongly in my youth, the moist smell of newly opened
earth, the chalky whitewash on the picket fence. It
must be. I do not believe in hobgoblins, ghosts, or
premonitions. No, it does not bear thinking about.
Foolishness! Let me get on with my story.

—When the great ships landed, I was feasting on
my grandfather's brains. All his descendants gathered
respectfully about him, and I, as youngest, had first
bite. His wisdom flowed through me, and the wisdom
of his ancestors and the intimate knowledge of those
animals he had eaten for food, and the spirit of valiant
enemies who had been killed and then honored by
being eaten, just as if they were family. I don't suppose
you understand this, little one.

I shook my head.

People never die, you see. Only humans die. Sometimes a minor part of a Person is lost, the doings of
a few decades, but the bulk of his life is preserved, if
not in this body, then in another. Or sometimes a
Person will dishonor himself, and his descendants will
refuse to eat him. This is a great shame, and the
Person will go off to die somewhere alone.

The ships descended bright as newborn suns. The
People had never seen such a thing. We watched in
inarticulate wonder, for we had no language then.

You have seen the pictures, the baroque swirls of colored metal, the proud humans stepping down onto the land. But I was there, and I can tell you, your people were ill. They stumbled down the gangplanks with the stench of radiation sickness about them. We could have destroyed them all then and there.

Your people built a village at Landfall and planted crops over the bodies of their dead. We left them alone. They did not look like good game. They were too strange and too slow and we had not yet come to savor your smell. So we went away, in baffled ignorance.

That was in early spring.

Half the survivors were dead by midwinter, some of disease but most because they did not have enough food. It was of no concern to us. But then the woman in the wilderness came to change our universe forever.

When you're older you'll be taught the woman's tale, and what desperation drove her into the wilderness. It's part of your history. But to myself, out in the mountains and winter-lean, the sight of her striding through the snows in her furs was like a vision of winter's queen herself. A gift of meat for the hungering season, life's blood for the solstice.

I first saw the woman while I was eating her mate. He had emerged from his cabin that evening as he did every sunset, gun in hand, without looking up. I had observed him over the course of five days and his behavior never varied. On that sixth nightfall I was crouched on his roof when he came out. I let him go a few steps from the door, then leapt. I felt his neck break on impact, tore open his throat to be sure, and ripped through his parka to taste his innards. There was no sport in it, but in winter we will take game whose brains we would never eat.

My mouth was full and my muzzle pleasantly, warmly moist with blood when the woman appeared. I looked up, and she was topping the rise, riding one of your incomprehensible machines, what I know now to be a snowstrider. The setting sun broke through the clouds behind her and for an instant she was embedded in glory. Her shadow stretched narrow before her and touched me, a bridge of darkness between us. We looked in one another's eyes . . .

Magda topped the rise with a kind of grim, joyless satisfaction. I am now a hunter's woman, she thought to herself. We will always be welcome at Landfall for the meat we bring, but they will never speak civilly to me again. Good. I would choke on their sweet talk anyway. The baby stirred and without looking down she stroked him through the furs, murmuring, "Just a little longer, my brave little boo, and we'll be at our new home. Will you like that, eh?"

The sun broke through the clouds to her back, making the snow a red dazzle. Then her eyes adjusted, and she saw the black shape crouched over her lover's body. A very great distance away, her hands throttled down the snowstrider and brought it to a halt. The shallow bowl of land before her was barren, the snow about the corpse black with blood. A last curl of smoke lazily separated from the hut's chimney. The brute lifted its bloody muzzle and looked at her.

Time froze and knotted in black agony.

The larl screamed. It ran straight at her, faster than thought. Clumsily, hampered by the infant strapped to her stomach, Magda clawed the rifle from its boot behind the saddle. She shucked her mittens, fitted hands to metal that stung like hornets, flicked off the safety and brought the stock to her shoulder. The larl was halfway to her. She aimed and fired.

The larl went down. One shoulder shattered, slamming it to the side. It tumbled and rolled in the snow. "You sonofabitch!" Magda cried in triumph. But almost immediately the beast struggled to its feet, turned and fled.

The baby began to cry, outraged by the rifle's roar. Magda powered up the engine. "Hush, small warrior." A kind of madness filled her, a blind anesthetizing rage. "This won't take long." She flung her machine downhill, after the larl.

Even wounded, the creature was fast. She could barely keep up. As it entered the spare stand of trees to the far end of the meadow, Magda paused to fire again, burning a bullet by its head. The larl leaped away. From then on it varied its flight with sudden changes of direction and unexpected jogs to the side. It was a fast learner. But it could not escape Magda. She had always been a hothead, and now her blood was up. She was not about to return to her lover's gutted body with his killer still alive.

The sun set and in the darkening light she lost sight of the larl. But she was able to follow its trail by two-shadowed moonlight, the deep, purple footprints, the darker spatter of blood it left, drop by drop, in the snow.

It was the solstice, and the moons were full—a holy time. I felt it even as I fled the woman through the wilderness. The moons were bright on the snow. I felt the dread of being hunted descend on me, and in my inarticulate way I felt blessed.

But I also felt a great fear for my kind. We had dismissed the humans as incomprehensible, not very interesting creatures, slow-moving, bad-smelling, and dull-witted. Now, pursued by this madwoman on her fast machine, brandishing a weapon that killed from afar, I felt all natural order betrayed. She was a goddess of the hunt, and I was her prey.

The People had to be told.

I gained distance from her, but I knew the woman would catch up. She was a hunter, and a hunter never abandons wounded prey. One way or another, she would have me.

In the winter, all who are injured or too old must offer themselves to the community. The sacrifice rock was not far, by a hill riddled from time beyond memory with our burrows. My knowledge must be shared: The humans were dangerous. They would make good prey.

I reached my goal when the moons were highest. The flat rock was bare of snow when I ran limping in. Awakened by the scent of my blood, several People emerged from their dens. I laid myself down on the sacrifice rock. A grandmother of the People came forward, licked my wound, tasting, considering. Then she nudged me away with her forehead. The wound would heal, she thought, and winter was young; my flesh was not yet needed.

But I stayed. Again she nudged me away. I refused to go. She whined in puzzlement. I licked the rock.

That was understood. Two of the People came forward and placed their weight on me. A third lifted a paw. He shattered my skull, and they ate.

* * *

Magda watched through power binoculars from atop a nearby ridge. She saw everything. The rock swarmed with lean black horrors. It would be dangerous to go down among them, so she waited and watched the puzzling tableau below. The larl had wanted to die, she'd swear it, and now the beasts came forward daintily, almost ritualistically, to taste the brains, the young first and then the old. She raised her rifle, thinking to exterminate a few of the brutes from afar.

A curious thing happened then. All the larls that had eaten of her prey's brain leaped away, scattering. Those that had not eaten waited, easy targets, not understanding. Then another dipped to lap up a fragment of brain, and looked up with sudden comprehension. Fear touched her.

The hunter had spoken often of the larls, had said that they were so elusive he sometimes thought them intelligent. "Come spring, when I can afford to waste ammunition on carnivores, I look forward to harvesting a few of these beauties," he'd said. He was the colony's xenobiologist, and he loved the animals he killed, treasured them even as he smoked their flesh, tanned their hides, and drew detailed pictures of their internal organs. Magda had always scoffed at his theory that larls gained insight into the habits of their prey by eating their brains, even though he'd spent much time observing the animals minutely from afar, gathering evidence. Now she wondered if he were right.

Her baby whimpered, and she slid a hand inside her furs to give him a breast. Suddenly the night seemed cold and dangerous, and she thought: What am I doing here? Sanity returned to her all at once, her anger collapsing to nothing, like an ice tower shattering in the wind. Below, sleek black shapes sped toward her, across the snow. They changed direction every few leaps, running evasive patterns to avoid her fire.

"Hang on, kid," she muttered, and turned her strider around. She opened up the throttle.

Magda kept to the open as much as she could, the creatures following her from a distance. Twice she stopped abruptly and turned her rifle on her pursuers. Instantly they disappeared in puffs of snow, crouching belly-down but not stopping, burrowing toward her under the surface. In the eerie night silence, she could hear the whispering sound of the brutes tunneling. She fled.

Some frantic timeless period later—the sky had still not lightened in the east—Magda was leaping a frozen stream when the strider's left ski struck a rock. The machine was knocked glancingly upward, cybernetics screaming as they fought to regain balance. With a sickening crunch, the strider slammed to earth, one ski twisted and bent. It would take extensive work before the strider could move again.

Magda dismounted. She opened her robe and looked down on her child. He smiled up at her and made a gurgling noise.

Something went dead in her.

A fool. I've been a criminal fool, she thought. Magda was a proud woman who had always refused to regret, even privately, anything she had done. Now she regretted everything: Her anger, the hunter, her entire life, all that had brought her to this point, the cumulative madness that threatened to kill her child.

A larl topped the ridge.

Magda raised her rifle, and it ducked down. She began walking down-slope, parallel to the stream. The snow was knee deep and she had to walk carefully not to slip and fall. Small pellets of snow rolled down ahead of her, were overtaken by other pellets. She strode ahead, pushing up a wake.

The hunter's cabin was not many miles distant; if she could reach it, they would live. But a mile was a long way in winter. She could hear the larls calling to each other, soft coughlike noises, to either side of the ravine. They were following the sound of her passage through the snow. Well, let them. She still had the rifle, and if it had few bullets left, *they* didn't know that. They were only animals.

This high in the mountains, the trees were sparse. Magda descended a good quarter-mile before the ravine choked with scrub and she had to climb up and out or risk being ambushed. Which way? she wondered. She heard three coughs to her right, and climbed the left slope, alert and wary.

We herded her. Through the long night we gave her fleeting glimpses of our bodies whenever she started to turn to the side she must not go, and let her pass unmolested the other way. We let her see us dig into the distant snow and wait motionless, undetectable. We filled the woods with our shadows. Slowly, slowly, we turned her around. She struggled to return to the cabin, but she could not. In what haze of fear and despair she walked! We could smell it. Sometimes her baby cried, and she hushed the milky-scented creature in a voice gone flat with futility. The night deepened as the moons sank in the sky. We forced the woman back up into the mountains. Toward the end, her legs failed her several times; she lacked our strength and stamina. But her patience and guile were every bit our match. Once we approached her still form, and she killed two of us before the rest could retreat. How we loved her! We paced her, confident that sooner or later she'd drop.

It was at night's darkest hour that the woman was forced back to the burrowed hillside, the sacred place of the People where stood the sacrifice rock. She topped the same rise for the second time that night, and saw it. For a moment she stood helpless, and then she burst into tears.

We waited, for this was the holiest moment of the hunt, the point when the prey recognizes and accepts her destiny. After a time, the woman's sobs ceased. She raised her head and straightened her back.

Slowly, steadily, she walked downhill.

She knew what to do.

Larls retreated into their burrows at the sight of her, gleaming eyes dissolving into darkness. Magda ignored them. Numb and aching, weary to death, she walked to the sacrifice rock. It had to be this way.

Magda opened her coat, unstrapped her baby. She wrapped him deep in the furs and laid the bundle down to one side of the rock. Dizzily, she opened the bundle to kiss the top of his sweet head, and he made an angry sound. "Good for you, kid," she said hoarsely. "Keep that attitude." She was so tired.

She took off her sweaters, her vest, her blouse. The raw cold nipped at her flesh with teeth of ice. She stretched slightly, body aching with motion. God it felt good. She laid down the rifle. She knelt.

The rock was black with dried blood. She lay down

flat, as she had earlier seen her larl do. The stone was cold, so cold it almost blanked out the pain. Her pursuers waited nearby, curious to see what she was doing; she could hear the soft panting noise of their breathing. One padded noiselessly to her side. She could smell the brute. It whined questioningly.

She licked the rock.

Once it was understood what the woman wanted, her sacrifice went quickly. I raised a paw, smashed her skull. Again I was youngest. Innocent, I bent to taste.

The neighbors were gathering, hammering at the door, climbing over one another to peer through the windows, making the walls bulge and breathe with their eagerness. I grunted and bellowed, and the clash of silver and clink of plates next door grew louder. Like peasant animals, my husband's people tried to drown out the sound of my pain with toasts and drunken jokes.

Through the window I saw Tevin-the-Fool's bone-white skin gaunt on his skull, and behind him a slice of face—sharp nose, white cheeks—like a mask. The doors and walls pulsed with the weight of those outside. In the next room, children fought and wrestled, and elders pulled at their long white beards, staring anxiously at the closed door.

The midwife shook her head, red lines running from the corners of her mouth down either side of her stern chin. Her eye sockets were shadowy pools of dust. "Now push!" she cried. "Don't be a lazy sow!"

I groaned and arched my back. I shoved my head back and it grew smaller, eaten up by the pillows. The bedframe skewed as one leg slowly buckled under it.

My husband glanced over his shoulder at me, an angry look, his fingers knotted behind his back.

All of Landfall shouted and hovered on the walls.

"Here it comes!" shrieked the midwife. She reached down to my bloody crotch, and eased out a tiny head, purple and angry, like a goblin.

And then all the walls glowed red and green and sprouted large flowers. The door turned orange and burst open, and the neighbors and crew flooded in. The ceiling billowed up, and aerialists tumbled through the rafters. A boy who had been hiding beneath the bed flew up laughing to where the ancient sky and stars shone through the roof.

They held up the child, bloody on a platter.

Here the larl touched me for the first time, that heavy black paw like velvet on my knee, talons sheathed. "Are you following this?" he asked. "Can you separate truth from fantasy, tell what is fact and what the mad imagery of emotions we did not share? No more could I. All that, the first birth of human young on this planet, I experienced in an instant. Blind with awe, I understood the personal tragedy and the communal triumph of that event, and the meaning of the lives and culture behind it. A second before, I lived as an animal, with an animal's simple thoughts and hopes. Then I ate of your ancestor and was lifted all in an instant halfway to godhood.

"As the woman had intended. She had died thinking of the child's birth, in order that we might share in it. She gave us that. She gave us more. She gave us *language*. We were wise animals before we ate her brain, and we were People afterward. We owed her

so much. And we knew what she wanted from us."
The larl stroked my cheek with his great, smooth paw,
the ivory claws hooded but quivering slightly, as if
about to awake.

I hardly dared breathe.

"That morning I entered Landfall, carrying the baby's sling in my mouth. It slept through most of the
journey. At dawn I passed through the empty street
as silently as I knew how. I came to the First Captain's
house. I heard the murmur of voices within, the entire
village assembled for worship. I tapped the door with
one paw. There was sudden, astonished silence. Then
slowly, fearfully, the door opened."

The larl was silent for a moment. "That was the
beginning of the association of People with humans.
We were welcomed into your homes, and we helped
with the hunting. It was a fair trade. Our food saved
many lives that first winter. No one needed know how
the woman had perished, or how well we understood
your kind.

"That child, Flip, was your ancestor. Every few generations we take one of your family out hunting, and
taste his brains, to maintain our closeness with your
line. If you are a good boy and grow up to be as bold
and honest, as intelligent and noble a man as your
father, then perhaps it will be you we eat."

The larl presented his blunt muzzle to me in what
might have been meant as a friendly smile. Perhaps
not; the expression hangs unreadable, ambiguous in
my mind even now. Then he stood and padded away
into the friendly dark shadows of the Stone House.

I was sitting staring into the coals a few minutes
later when my second-eldest sister—her face a fea-

tureless blaze of light, like an angel's—came into the room and saw me. She held out a hand, saying, "Come on, Flip, you're missing everything." And I went with her.

Did any of this actually happen? Sometimes I wonder. But it's growing late, and your parents are away. My room is small but snug, my bed warm but empty. We can burrow deep in the blankets and scare away the cave-bears by playing the oldest winter games there are.

You're blushing! Don't tug away your hand. I'll be gone soon to some distant world to fight in a war for people who are as unknown to you as they are to me. Soldiers grow old slowly, you know. We're shipped frozen between the stars. When you are old and plump and happily surrounded by grandchildren, I'll still be young, and thinking of you. You'll remember me then, and our thoughts will touch in the void. Will you have nothing to regret? Is that really what you want?

I thought once that I could outrun the darkness. I thought—I must have thought—that by joining the militia I could escape my fate. But for all that I gave up my home and family, in the end the beast came anyway to eat my brain. Now I am alone. A month from now, in all this world, only you will remember my name. Let me live in your memory.

Come, don't be shy. Let's put the past aside and get on with our lives. That's better. Blow the candle out, love, and there's an end to my tale.

All this happened long ago, on a planet whose name has been burned from my memory.

Christmas on Ganymede

Isaac Asimov

Olaf Johnson hummed nasally to himself and his china-blue eyes were dreamy as he surveyed the stately fir tree in the corner of the library. Though the library was the largest single room in the Dome, Olaf felt it none too spacious for the occasion. Enthusiastically he dipped into the huge crate at his side and took out the first roll of red-and-green crêpe paper.

What sudden burst of sentiment had inspired the Ganymedan Products Corporation, Inc. to ship a complete collection of Christmas decorations to the Dome, he did not pause to inquire. Olaf's was a placid disposition, and in his self-imposed job as chief Christmas decorator, he was content with his lot.

He frowned suddenly and muttered a curse. The General Assembly signal light was flashing on and off hysterically. With a hurt air Olaf laid down the tack-hammer he had just lifted, then the roll of crêpe paper, picked some tinsel out of his hair and left for officers quarters.

Commander Scott Pelham was in his deep armchair at the head of the table when Olaf entered. His stubby fingers were drumming unrhythmically upon the glass-topped table. Olaf met the commander's hotly furious eyes without fear, for nothing had gone wrong in his department in twenty Ganymedan revolutions.

The room filled rapidly with men, and Pelham's eyes hardened as he counted noses in one sweeping glance.

"We're all here. Men, we face a crisis!"

There was a vague stir. Olaf's eyes sought the ceiling and he relaxed. Crises hit the Dome once a revolution, on the average. Usually they turned out to be a sudden rise in the quota of oxite to be gathered, or the inferior quality of the last batch of karen leaves. He stiffened, however, at the next words.

"In connection with the crisis, I have one question to ask." Pelham's voice was a deep baritone, and it rasped unpleasantly when he was angry. "What dirty imbecilic troublemaker has been telling those blasted Ossies fairy tales?"

Olaf cleared his throat nervously and thus immediately became the center of attention. His Adam's apple wobbled in sudden alarm and his forehead wrinkled into a washboard. He shivered.

"I—I—" he stuttered, quickly fell silent. His long fingers made a bewildered gesture of appeal. "I mean I was out there yesterday, after the last—uh—supplies of karen leaves, on account the Ossies were slow and—"

A deceptive sweetness entered Pelham's voice. He smiled.

"Did you tell those natives about Santa Claus, Olaf?"

The smile looked uncommonly like a wolfish leer and Olaf broke down. He nodded convulsively.

"Oh, you did? Well, well, you told them about Santa Claus! He comes down in a sleigh that flies through the air with eight reindeer pulling it, huh?"

"Well—er—doesn't he?" Olaf asked unhappily.

"And you drew pictures of the reindeer, just to make sure there was no mistake. Also, he has a long white beard and red clothes with white trimmings."

"Yeah, that's right," said Olaf, his face puzzled.

"And he has a big bag, chock full of presents for good little boys and girls, and he brings it down the chimney and puts presents inside stockings."

"Sure."

"You also told them he's about due, didn't you? One more revolution and he's going to visit us."

Olaf smiled weakly. "Yeah, Commander, I meant to tell you. I'm fixing up the tree and—"

"Shut up!" The commander was breathing hard in a whistling sort of way. "Do you know what those Ossies have thought of?"

"No, Commander."

Pelham leaned across the table toward Olaf and shouted:

"They want Santa Claus to visit *them!*"

Someone laughed and changed it quickly into a strangling cough at the commander's raging stare.

"And if Santa Claus doesn't visit them, the Ossies are going to quit work!" He repeated, "Quit cold—strike!"

There was no laughter, strangled or otherwise, after that. If there were more than one thought am ng the entire group, it didn't show itself. Olaf expressed that thought:

"But what about the quota?"

"Well, what about it?" snarled Pelham. "Do I have to draw pictures for you? Ganymedan Products has to get one hundred tons of wolframite, eighty tons of karen leaves and fifty tons of oxite every year, or it loses its franchise. I suppose there isn't anyone here who doesn't know that. It so happens that the current year ends in two Ganymedan revolutions, and we're five per cent behind schedule as it is."

There was pure, horrified silence.

"And now the Ossies won't work unless they get Santa Claus. No work, no quota, no franchise—no jobs! Get that, you low-grade morons. When the company loses its franchise, we lose the best-paying jobs in the System. Kiss them good-by, men, unless—"

He paused, glared steadily at Olaf, and added:

"Unless, by next revolution, we have a flying sleigh, eight reindeer and a Santa Claus. And by every cosmic speck in the rings of Saturn, we're going to have just that, especially a Santa!"

Ten faces turned ghastly pale.

"Got someone in mind, Commander?" asked someone in a voice that was three-quarters croak.

"Yes, as a matter of fact, I have."

He sprawled back in his chair. Olaf Johnson broke into a sudden sweat as he found himself staring at the end of a pointing forefinger.

"Aw, Commander!" he quavered.

The pointing finger never moved.

* * *

Pelham tramped into the foreroom, removed his oxygen nosepiece and the cold cylinders attached to it. One by one he cast off thick woolen outer garments and, with a final, weary sigh, jerked off a pair of heavy knee-high space boots.

Sim Pierce paused in his careful inspection of the latest batch of karen leaves and cast a hopeful glance over his spectacles.

"Well?" he asked.

Pelham shrugged. "I promised them Santa. What else could I do? I also doubled sugar rations, so they're back on the job—for the moment."

"You mean till the Santa we promised doesn't show up." Pierce straightened and waved a long karen leaf at the commander's face for emphasis. "This is the silliest thing I ever heard of. It can't be done. There ain't no Santa Claus!"

"Try telling that to the Ossies." Pelham slumped into a chair and his expression became stonily bleak. "What's Benson doing?"

"You mean that flying sleigh he says he can rig up?" Pierce held a leaf up to the light and peered at it critically. "He's a crackpot, if you ask me. The old buzzard went down to the sub-level this morning and he's been there ever since. All I know is that he's taken the spare lectro-dissociator apart. If anything happens to the regular, it just means that we're without oxygen."

"Well," Pelham rose heavily, "for my part I hope we *do* choke. It would be an easy way out of this whole mess. I'm going down below."

He stumped out and slammed the door behind him.

In the sub-level he gazed about in bewilderment, for the room was littered with gleaming chrome-steel machine parts. It took him some time to recognize the mess as the remains of what had been a compact, snugly built lectro-dissociator the day before. In the center, in anachronistic contrast, stood a dusty wooden sleigh atop rust-red runners. From beneath it came the sound of hammering.

"Hey, Benson!" called Pelham.

A grimy, sweat-streaked face pushed out from underneath the sleigh, and a stream of tobacco juice shot toward Benson's ever-present cuspidor.

"What are you shouting like that for?" he complained. "This is delicate work."

"What the devil is that weird contraption?" demanded Pelham.

"Flying sleigh. My own idea, too." The light of enthusiasm shone in Benson's watery eyes, and the quid in his mouth shifted from cheek to cheek as he spoke. "The sleigh was brought here in the old days, when they thought Ganymede was covered with snow like the other Jovian moons. All I have to do is fix a few gravo-repulsors from the dissociator to the bottom and that'll make it weightless when the current's on. Compressed air-jets will do the rest."

The commander chewed his lower lip dubiously.

"Will it work?"

"Sure it will. Lots of people have thought of using repulsors in air travel, but they're inefficient, especially in heavy gravity fields. Here on Ganymede, with a field of one-third gravity and a thin atmosphere, a child could run it. Even Johnson could run it, though I wouldn't mourn if he fell off and broke his blasted neck."

"All right, then, look here. We've got lots of this native purplewood. Get Charlie Finn and tell him to put that sleigh on a platform of it. He's to have it extend about twenty feet or more frontward, with a railing around the part that projects."

Benson spat and scowled through the stringy hair over his eyes.

"What's the idea, Commander?"

Pelham's laughter came in short, harsh barks.

"Those Ossies are expecting reindeer, and reindeer they're going to have. Those animals will have to stand on something, won't they?"

"Sure . . . But wait, hold on! There aren't any reindeer on Ganymede."

Commander Pelham paused on his way out. His eyes narrowed unpleasantly as they always did when he thought of Olaf Johnson.

"Olaf is out rounding up eight spinybacks for us. They've got four feet, a head on one end and a tail on the other. That's close enough for the Ossies."

The old engineer chewed this information and chuckled nastily.

"Good! I wish the fool joy of his job."

"So do I," gritted Pelham.

He stalked out as Benson, still leering, slid underneath the sleigh.

The commander's description of a spinyback was concise and accurate, but it left out several interesting details. For one thing, a spinyback has a long, mobile snout, two large ears that wave back and forth gently, and two emotional purple eyes. The males have pliable spines of a deep crimson color along the backbone that seem to delight the female of the species. Combine these with a scaly, muscular tail and a brain by no means mediocre, and you have a spinyback—

or at least you have one if you can catch one.

It was just such a thought that occurred to Olaf Johnson as he sneaked down from the rocky eminence toward the herd of twenty-five spinybacks grazing on the sparse, gritty undergrowth. The nearest spinies looked up as Olaf, bundled in fur and grotesque with attached oxygen nosepiece, approached. However, spinies have no natural enemies, so they merely gazed at the figure with languidly disapproving eyes and returned to their crunchy but nourishing fare.

Olaf's notions on bagging big game were sketchy. He fumbled in his pocket for a lump of sugar, held it out and said:

"Here, pussy, pussy, pussy, pussy, pussy!"

The ears of the nearest spinie twitched in annoyance. Olaf came closer and held out the sugar again.

"Come, bossy! Come, bossy!"

The spinie caught sight of the sugar and rolled his eyes at it. His snout twitched as he spat out his last mouthful of vegetation and ambled over. With neck stretched out, he sniffed. Then, using a rapid, expert motion, he struck at the outheld palm and flipped the lump into his mouth. Olaf's other hand whistled down upon nothingness.

With a hurt expression, Olaf held out another piece.

"Here, Prince! Here, Fido!"

The spinie made a low, tremulous sound deep in his throat. It was a sound of pleasure. Evidently this strange monstrosity before him, having gone insane, intended to feed him these bits of concentrated succulence forever. He snatched and was back as quickly as the first time. But, since Olaf had held on firmly this time, the spinie almost bagged half a finger as well.

Olaf's yell lacked a bit of the nonchalance necessary at such times. Nevertheless, a bite that can be felt through thick gloves is a *bite!*

He advanced boldly upon the spinie. There are some things that stir the Johnson blood and bring up the ancient spirit of the Vikings. Having one's finger bitten, especially by an unearthly animal, is one of these.

There was an uncertain look in the spinie's eyes as he backed slowly away. There weren't any white cubes being offered any more and he wasn't quite sure what was going to happen now. The uncertainty vanished with a suddenness he did not expect, when two glove-muffled hands came down upon his ears and jerked. He let out a high-pitched yelp and charged forward.

A spinie has a certain sense of dignity. He doesn't like to have his ears pulled, particularly when other spinies, including several unattached females, have formed a ring and are looking on.

The Earthman went over backward and remained in that position for awhile. Meantime, the spinie backed away a few feet in a gentlemanly manner and allowed Johnson to get to his feet.

The old Viking blood frothed still higher in Olaf. After rubbing the hurt spot where he had landed on his oxygen cylinder, he jumped, forgetting to allow for Ganymedan gravity. He sailed five feet over the spinie's back.

There was awe in the animal's eye as he watched Olaf, for it was a stately jump. But there was a certain amount of bewilderment as well. There seemed to be no purpose to the maneuver.

Olaf landed on his back again and got the cylinder

in the same place. He was beginning to feel a little embarrassed. The sounds that came from the circle of onlookers were remarkably like snickers.

"Laugh!" he muttered bitterly. "I haven't even begun to fight yet."

He approached the spinie slowly, cautiously. He circled, watching for his opening. So did the spinie. Olaf feinted and the spinie ducked. Then the spinie reared and Olaf ducked.

Olaf kept remembering new profanity all the time. The husky "Ur-r-r-r" that came out the spinie's throat seemed to lack the brotherly spirit that is usually associated with Christmas.

There was a sudden, swishing sound. Olaf felt something collide with his skull, just behind his left ear. This time he turned a back somersault and landed on the nape of his neck. There was a chorused whinny from the onlookers, and the spinie waved his tail triumphantly.

Olaf got rid of the impression that he was floating through a star-studded unlimited space and wavered to his feet.

"Listen," he objected, "using your tail is a foul!"

He leaped back as the tail shot forward again, then flung himself forward in a diving tackle. He grabbed at the spinie's feet and felt the animal come down on his back with an indignant yelp.

Now it was a case of Earth muscles against Ganymedan muscles, and Olaf became a man of brute strength. He struggled up, and the spinie found himself slung over the stranger's shoulders.

The spinie objected vociferously and tried to prove his objections by a judicious whip of the tail. But he was in an inconvenient position and the stroke whistled harmlessly over Olaf's head.

The other spinies made way for the Earthman with saddened expressions. Evidently they were all good friends of the captured animal and hated to see him lose a fight. They returned to their meal in philosophic resignation, plainly convinced that it was kismet.

On the other side of the rocky ledge, Olaf reached his prepared cave. There was the briefest of scrambling struggles before he managed to sit down hard on the spinie's head and put enough knots into rope to hold him there.

A few hours later, when he had corralled his eighth spinyback, he possessed the technique that comes of long practice. He could have given a Terrestrial cowboy valuable pointers on throwing a maverick. Also, he could have given a Terrestrial stevedore lessons in simple and compound swearing.

'Twas the night before Christmas—and all through the Ganymedan Dome there was deafening noise and bewildering excitement, like an exploding nova equipped for sound. Around the rusty sleigh, mounted on its huge platform of purplewood, five Earthmen were staging a battle royal with a spinie.

The spinie had definite views about most things, and one of his stubbornest and most definite views was that he would never go where he didn't want to go. He made that clear by flailing one head, one tail, three spines and four legs in every possible direction, with all possible force.

But the Earthmen insisted, and not gently. Despite loud, agonized squeaks, the spinie was lifted onto the platform, hauled into place and harnessed into hopeless helplessness.

"Okay!" Peter Benson yelled. "Pass the bottle."

Holding the spinie's snout with one hand, Benson waved the bottle under it with the other. The spinie quivered eagerly and whined tremulously. Benson poured some of the liquid down the animal's throat. There was a gurgling swallow and an appreciative whinny. The spinie's neck stretched out for more.

Benson sighed. "Our best brandy, too."

He up-ended the bottle and withdrew it half empty. The spinie, eyes whirling in their sockets rapidly, did what seemed an attempt at a gay jig. It didn't last long, however, for Ganymedan metabolism is almost immediately affected by alcohol. His muscles locked in a drunken rigor and, with a loud hiccup, he went out on his feet.

"Drag out the next!" yelled Benson.

In an hour the eight spinybacks were so many cataleptic statues. Forked sticks were tied around their heads as antlers. The effect was crude and sketchy, but it would do.

As Benson opened his mouth to ask where Olaf Johnson was, that worthy showed up in the arms of three comrades, and he was putting up as stiff a fight as any spinie. His objections, however, were highly articulate.

"I'm not going anywhere in this costume!" he roared, gouging at the nearest eye. "You hear me?"

There certainly was cause for objection. Even at his best, Olaf had never been a heart-throb. But in his present condition, he resembled a hybrid between a spinie's nightmare and a Picassian conception of a patriarch.

He wore the conventional costume of Santa. His clothes were as red as red tissue paper sewed onto his space coat could make it. The "ermine" was as white as cotton wool, which it was. His beard, more cotton wool glued into a linen foundation, hung loosely from his ears. With that below and his oxygen nosepiece above, even the strongest were forced to avert their eyes.

Olaf had not been shown a mirror. But, between what he could see of himself and what his instinct told him, he would have greeted a good, bright lightning bolt like a brother.

By fits and starts, he was hauled to the sleigh. Others pitched in to help, until Olaf was nothing but a smothered squirm and muffled voice.

"Leggo," he mumbled. "Leggo and come at me one by one. Come on!"

He tried to spar a bit, to point his dare. But the multiple grips upon him left him unable to wriggle a finger.

"Get in!" ordered Benson.

"You go to hell!" gasped Olaf. "I'm not getting into any patented short-cut to suicide, and you can take your bloody flying sleigh and—"

"Listen," interrupted Benson, "Commander Pelham is waiting for you at the other end. He'll skin you alive if you don't show up in half an hour."

"Commander Pelham can take the sleigh sideways and—"

"Then think of your job! Think of a hundred and fifty a week. Think of every other year off with pay. Think of Hilda, back on Earth, who isn't going to marry you without a job. Think of all that!"

Johnson thought, snarled. He thought some more, got into the sleigh, strapped down his bag and turned

on the gravo-repulsors. With a horrible curse, he
opened the rear jet.

The sleigh dashed forward and he caught himself
from going backward, over and out of the sleigh, by
two-thirds of a whisker. He held onto the sides there-
after, watching the surrounding hills as they rose and
fell with each lurch of the unsteady sleigh.

As the wind rose, the undulations grew more
marked. And when Jupiter came up, its yellow light
brought out every jag and crag of the rocky ground,
toward every one of which, in turn, the sleigh seemed
headed. And by the time the giant planet had shoved
completely over the horizon, the curse of drink—
which departs from the Ganymedan organism just as
quickly as it descends—began removing itself from
the spinies.

The hindmost spinie came out of it first, tasted the
inside of his mouth, winced and swore off drink. Having made that resolution, he took in his immediate
surroundings languidly. They made no immediate
impression on him. Only gradually was the fact forced
upon him that his footing, whatever it was, was not
the usual stable one of solid Ganymede. It swayed and
shifted, which seemed very unusual.

Yet he might have attributed this unsteadiness to
his recent orgy, had he not been so careless as to drop
his glance over the railing to which he was anchored.
No spinie ever died of heart-failure, as far as is recorded, but, looking downward, this one almost did.

His agonized screech of horror and despair brought
the other spinies into full, if headachy, consciousness.
For a while there was a confused blur of squawking
conversation as the animals tried to get the pain out
of their heads and the facts in. Both aims were

achieved and a stampede was organized. It wasn't much of a stampede, because the spinies were anchored tightly. But, except for the fact that they got nowhere, they went through all the motions of a full gallop. And the sleigh went crazy.

Olaf grabbed his beard a second before it let go of his ears.

"Hey!" he shouted.

It was something like saying "Tut, tut" to a hurricane.

The sleigh kicked, bucked and did a hysterical tango. It made sudden spurts, as if inspired to dash its wooden brains out against Ganymede's crust. Meanwhile Olaf prayed, swore, wept and jiggled all the compressed air jets at once.

Ganymede whirled and Jupiter was a wild blur. Perhaps it was the spectacle of Jupiter doing the shimmy that steadied the spinies. More likely it was the fact that they just didn't give a hang any more. Whatever it was, they halted, made lofty farewell speeches to one another, confessed their sins and waited for death.

The sleigh steadied and Olaf resumed his breathing once more. Only to stop again as he viewed the curious spectacle of hills and solid ground up above, and black sky and swollen Jupiter down below.

It was at this point that he, too, made his peace with the eternal and awaited the end.

"Ossie" is short for ostrich, and that's what native Ganymedans look like, except that their necks are shorter, their heads are larger, and their feathers look as if they were about to fall out by the roots. To this, add a pair of scrawny, feathered arms with three stubby fingers apiece. They can speak English, but when you hear them, you wish they couldn't.

There were fifty of them in the low purplewood structure that was their "meeting hall." On the mound of raised dirt in the front of the room—dark with the smoky dimness of burning purplewood torches fetid to boot—sat Commander Scott Pelham and five of his men. Before them strutted the frowziest Ossie of them all, inflating his huge chest with rhythmic, booming sounds.

He stopped for a moment and pointed to a ragged hole in the ceiling.

"Look!" he squawked. "Chimney. We make. Sannycaws come in."

Pelham grunted approval. The Ossie clucked happily. He pointed to the little sacks of woven grass that hung from the walls.

"Look! Stockies. Sannycaws put presets!"

"Yeah," said Pelham unenthusiastically. "Chimney and stockings. Very nice." He spoke out of the corner of his mouth to Sim Pierce, who sat next to him: "Another half-hour in this dump will kill me. When is that fool coming?"

Pierce stirred uneasily.

"Listen," he said, "I've been doing some figuring. We're safe on everything but the karen leaves, and we're still four tons short on that. If we can get this fool business over with in the next hour, so we can start the next shift and work the Ossies at double, we can make it." He leaned back. "Yes, I think we can make it."

"Just about," replied Pelham gloomily. "That's if Johnson gets here without pulling another bloomer."

The Ossie was talking again, for Ossie like to talk. He said:

"Every year Kissmess comes. Kissmess nice, evvy-body friendly. Ossie like Kissmess. You like Kissmess?"

"Yeah, fine," Pelham snarled politely. "Peace on Ganymede, good will toward men—especially Johnson. Where the devil is that idiot, anyhow?"

He fell into an annoyed fidget, while the Ossie jumped up and down a few times in a thoughtful sort of manner, evidently for the exercise of it. He continued the jumping, varying it with little hopping dance steps, till Pelham's fists began making strangling gestures. Only an excited squawk from the hole in the wall dignified by the term "window" kept Pelham from committing Ossie-slaughter.

Ossies swarmed about and the Earthmen fought for a view.

Against Jupiter's great yellowness was outlined a flying sleigh, complete with reindeers. It was only a tiny thing, but there was no doubt about it. Santa Claus was coming.

There was only one thing wrong with the picture. The sleigh, "reindeer" and all, while plunging ahead at a terrific speed, was flying upside down.

The Ossies dissolved into squawking cacophony.

"Sannycaws! Sannycaws! Sannycaws!"

They scrambled out the window like so many animated dust-mops gone mad. Pelham and his men used the low door.

The sleigh was approaching, growing larger, lurching from side to side and vibrating like an off-center flywheel. Olaf Johnson was a tiny figure holding on desperately to the side of the sleigh with both hands.

Pelham was shouting wildly, incoherently, choking on the thin atmosphere every time he forgot to breathe through his nose. Then he stopped and stared in horror. The sleigh, almost life-size now, was dipping down. If it had been an arrow shot by William Tell, it could not have aimed between Pelham's eyes more accurately.

"Everybody down!" he shrieked, and dropped.

The wind of the sleigh's passage whistled keenly and brushed his face. Olaf's voice could be heard for an instant, high-pitched and indistinct. Compressed air spurted, leaving tracks of condensing water vapor.

Pelham lay quivering, hugging Ganymede's frozen crust. Then, knees shaking like a Hawaiian hula-girl, he rose slowly. The Ossies who had scattered before the plunging vehicle had assembled again. Off in the distance, the sleigh was veering back.

Pelham watched as it swayed and hovered, still rotating. It lurched toward the dome, curved off to one side, turned back, and gathered speed.

Inside that sleigh, Olaf worked like a demon. Straddling his legs wide, he shifted his weight desperately. Sweating and cursing, trying hard not to look "downward" at Jupiter, he urged the sleigh into wilder and wilder swings. It was wobbling through an angle of 180 degrees now, and Olaf felt his stomach raise strenuous objections.

Holding his breath, he leaned hard with his right foot and felt the sleigh swing far over. At the extremity of that swing, he released the gravo-repulsor and, in Ganymede's weak gravity, the sleigh jerked downward. Naturally, since the vehicle was bottom-heavy due to the metal gravo-repulsor beneath, it righted itself as it fell.

But this was little comfort to Commander Pelham, who found himself once more in the direct path of the sleigh.

"Down!" he yelled, and dropped again.

The sleigh *whi-i-ished* overhead, came up against a huge boulder with a *crack*, bounced twenty-five feet into the air, came down with a *rush* and a *bang*, and Olaf fell over the railing and out.

Santa Claus had arrived.

With a deep, shuddering breath, Olaf swung his bag over his shoulders, adjusted his beard and patted one of the silently suffering spinies on the head. Death might be coming—in fact, Olaf could hardly wait—but he was going to die on his feet nobly, like a Johnson.

Inside the shack, into which the Ossies had once more swarmed, a *thump* announced the arrival of Santa's bag on the roof, and a second *thud* the arrival of Santa himself. A ghastly face appeared through the makeshift hole in the ceiling.

"Merry Christmas!" it croaked, and tumbled through.

Olaf landed on his oxygen cylinders, as usual, and got them in the usual place.

The Ossies jumped up and down like rubber balls with the itch.

Olaf limped heavily toward the first stocking and deposited the garishly colored sphere he withdrew from his bag, one of the many that had originally been intended as a Christmas tree ornament. One by one he deposited the rest in every available stocking.

Having completed his job, he dropped into an exhausted squat, from which position he watched subsequent proceedings with a glazed and fishy eye. The jolliness and belly-shaking good humor, traditionally characteristic of Santa Claus, were absent from this one with remarkable thoroughness.

The Ossies made up for it by their wild ecstasy. Until Olaf had deposited the last globe, they had kept their silence and their seats. But when he had finished, the air heaved and writhed under the stresses of the discordant screeches that arose. In half a second the hand of each Ossie contained a globe.

They chattered among themselves furiously, handling the globes carefully and hugging them close to their chests. Then they compared one with another, flocking about to gaze at particularly good ones.

The frowziest Ossie approached Pelham and plucked at the commander's sleeve. "Sannycaws good," he cackled. "Look, he leave eggs!" He stared reverently at his sphere and said: "Pittier'n Ossie eggs, huh?"

His skinny finger punched Pelham in the stomach.

"No!" yowled Pelham vehemently. "Hell, no!"

But the Ossie wasn't listening. He plunged the globe deep into the warmth of his feathers and said:

"Pitty colors. How long take for little Sannycaws come out? And what little Sannycaws eat?" He looked up. "We take good care. We teach little Sannycaws, make him smart and full of brain like Ossie."

Pierce grabbed Commander Pelham's arm.

"Don't argue with them," he whispered frantically. "What do you care if they think those are Santa Claus eggs? Come on! If we work like maniacs, we can still make the quota. Let's get started."

"That's right," Pelham admitted. He turned to the Ossie. "Tell everyone to get going." He spoke clearly and loudly. "Work now. Do you understand? Hurry, hurry, hurry! Come on!"

He motioned with his arms. But the frowzy Ossie had come to a sudden halt. He said slowly:

"We work, but Johnson say Kissmess come evvy year."

"Isn't one Christmas enough for you?" Pelham rasped.

"No!" squawked the Ossie. "We want Sannycaws next year. Get more eggs. And next year more eggs. And next year. And next year. And next year. More eggs. More little Sannycaws eggs. If Sannycaws not come, we not work."

"That's a long time off," said Pelham. "We'll talk about it then. By that time I'll either have gone completely crazy, or you'll have forgotten all about it."

Pierce opened his mouth, closed it, opened his mouth, closed it, opened it, and finally managed to speak.

"Commander, they want him to come every year."

"I know. They won't remember by next year, though."

"But you don't get it. A year to them is one Ganymedan revolution around Jupiter. In Earth time, that's seven days and three hours. They want Santa Claus to come every *week*."

"Every week!" Pelham gulped. "Johnson told them—"

For a moment everything turned sparkling somersaults before his eyes. He choked, and automatically his eye sought Olaf.

Olaf turned cold to the marrow of his bones and rose to his feet apprehensively, sidling toward the door. There he stopped as a sudden recollection of tradition hit him. Beard a-dangle, he croaked:

"Merry Christmas to all, and to all a good night!"

He made for the sleigh as if all the imps of Hades were after him. The imps weren't, but Commander Scott Pelham was.

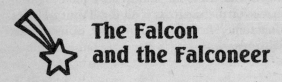

The Falcon
and the Falconeer

Barry N. Malzberg

Depositions taken after the event:

ROMANO, CHAPLAIN: The ways of the Deity are imponderable; the more intricate and vast the universe becomes to us, the more imponderable they must be. This is the kind of thing which must be understood; it has taken me forty years to learn it, and I cannot emphasize sufficiently how basic the point is. There was a time, I understand, at the advent of institutionalized science and the emergence of the rational ethic, when it was thought that the further and further we went, the more we learned; the longer we voyaged, the more the mysteries would dissipate until finally, ultimately, there would be a time when knowledge outweighed mystery totally and everything was controlled. It was only within the last few centuries, I think, that we began to realize it worked the other way; that we learned only to play out our madness and insufficiency on a larger canvas; that spacedrive and the colonization of the galaxy only meant that the uncontrollable had larger implications. At least, this is what I insist. Therefore, I feel no sense of guilt at what happened on Rigel XIV; it was not my responsibility. I did all that I could, of course, to discourage the disgusting adventure, but how much influence does a chaplain really have, particularly with men who have had almost to deny God to get where they are? I don't like this testimony any more than you like taking it, gentlemen, but one must face facts. In a difficult age, you must abandon preconception, posture, even hope, and do things in a difficult way. I have found this a life-sustaining rationalization.

Certainly I cautioned against it. I said to Williams the moment I heard about it and was able to gain access to him, "Captain Williams, I urge you to put an end to these plans. They are sacrilegious, they are abrupt, they are irrelevant, and they might even be actually dangerous. We should celebrate Christmas in the hallowed fashion, or we should not celebrate it at all, but we are not in any way directed to make a spectacle which can only be apostate. Besides, some of the more irreverent may be led to make remarks and come to conclusions which could only be justified under the circumstances. The idea of the crèche is bad enough, but populating it with living figures is even more disgusting. Besides, the atmosphere here is absolutely intolerable, and the men will be forced to don heavy spacegear if the ceremony takes any time whatsoever. And the Rigellians, while certainly affecting creatures in their own way, are unfortunately not of an appearance or manner which should be included in any serious religious ceremony. Aside from all the jokes which have been made about their physical aspect, they smell badly and they have a foul sense of humor."

Williams didn't listen, of course. There was no way he could. By the time I had managed to secure an appointment with him—a chaplain, as you are finding out, has very low rank on these survey teams—it was only two hours before the ceremony. There was no time to cancel, even if he had been disposed to do so anyway, which he said he was not. He said my ideas were laughable. He said that I was looking at things in a totally didactic and sentimental fashion. He said that the men in this far-flung outpost needed their entertainment any way they could get it, sex to the contrary, and that the fact that they had wanted to have a Christmas pageant indicated that they might even be able to make something serious out of it, along with the other parts. He got up and paced excitedly and finished off a bottle of whiskey, which he said he was drinking in his quarters to celebrate the occasion, and then he threw me out, politely, saying that he had to get ready for the ceremony himself since he had been enlisted to play the part of a Pharisee, a very great honor. I came in without hope and I left without despair. There was nothing that I could do. To the best of my ability I had stated my warning. Beyond that it could not be my responsibility.

As to the grievous events which followed and which resulted in all of us being here, I have nothing to say about them. I could have predicted it. We voyage further and further into the darkness, only to see the universe cleave and shriek under us. Of course. Of course. I furnished what moderate spiritual counseling that I could, and as far as the ceremony itself is concerned, I saw nothing of it. All that happened I derived only at third hand. You need only take it up, then, with those that were there. Why bother me, anyway? I realize that you need a religious expert to make a deposition, but I simply cannot help you, gentlemen, I have my own problems.

HAWKINS, BOTANY TECHNICIAN: Well, I guess lucky is the word for it. It could have been me. I was originally scheduled to play the role, only I changed my mind at the last moment, and they slipped Cullings in. Boy, was I horrified when I saw what happened to Cullings! It was like everything that was going on was happening to me, only I wasn't there. I ended up with a small role, tending one of the donkeys, which was bad enough under all the circumstances.

The reason I backed out at the last moment was because of Dr. Romano, the team chaplain, and I really appreciate everything that he did for me now, although I wasn't happy about it then. Just when the rehearsals were beginning, Dr. Romano came up to me and said he wanted to talk to me when I got a chance, and because I didn't want to get in any trouble—he was an officer, after all—I went to his room later on and we chatted a bit. He said he knew from looking up my record that I came from a religious background and under all the circumstances he wanted to know how I got involved in something like this. I told him that the reason I had volunteered to play the Child was exactly *because* of this religious background of mine; I had always taken this seriously and had had a good upbringing and taking the role

I did was like I was making a contribution to what I believed in. But then Dr. Romano explained to me that it wasn't so much of a religious thing as an apostasy, he called it, because the thing was being done only for entertainment and spectacle and not because most of the people involved believed in it at all, and I began to understand what he was trying to say to me. He said that in any situation at any time you were going to find people who were going to play upon faith and use its appearance rather than its meaning for purposes of their own, but the thing the truly religious man learned to do was to recognize it and avoid it. *Fight it with all his heart's might,* Dr. Romano said, or something like that. So I backed right out of playing the role; I felt bad about it, of course, because they had already fitted the garments for me and arranged things my way, but knowing what a fool I had almost been taken for, it was a guaranteed thing I wasn't going to do it. I took one of those small, supporting roles instead, and they slotted Cullings in because he was kind of the same size as I was and they didn't have to make too many changes. Actually, Cullings was happy to do it; the way it worked out it was a kind of an honor to play that role, which was another one of the reasons I was unhappy. But when I saw the way it worked out, I started being grateful, and I haven't stopped being grateful to this day.

No, of course I didn't understand what was going on there. What was there to understand? Who could know? How could it get over to us? It was just a game, a kind of game we were playing in that damned place because we were so bored and the natives there were so anxious to please and because Christmas was coming on. If it happened to me in some other way in some other place, I still wouldn't know what was going on. But it won't happen because I'm getting out of the service; my enlistment would have been up a week ago if it hadn't been for this hearing; and no matter what you do to us, I'm never going out there again. Even if I'm kept somewhere for thirty years. Because you reach a point when you finally reach a point, you know what I mean? I didn't know Cullings well at all; he was just a guy. There were a lot of us out there, you know; it was like a good-sized town and everybody had their own jobs and fitted in with the people who were working around them. I was sure sorry to see what happened, though.

XCBNMJY, NATIVE: The trumpet shall sound and the dead shall be raised incorruptible for behold I tell you a mystery we do not sleep but we shall all be changed in a moment in the twinkling of an eye at the last trumpet (transcript becomes illegible).

WILLIAMS, COMMANDER: I'll tell this as simply and straightforwardly as possible, and then I'll have nothing more to say. I think that a court of inquiry has been called on this sad incident is disgraceful. There is absolutely no reason for it, and were it not for the fact that certain elements of the bureaucracy felt their own positions to be obscurely threatened by the events, this never would have occurred. They're merely trying to hang us so they won't be touched. I was always a straightforward man, and I speak the truth. This is one of the hazards of command. What do those hacks and clerks know of responsibility?

Sure, I okayed the pageant. Rigel XIV is a dismal outpost, one of the worst assignments in the survey corps. The terrain is lousy; the view is impossible; the climate is intolerable; and to top it all off, the atmosphere, which seems perfectly benign on first exposure, turns out to kill you if you're exposed to it for more than thirty minutes. That was found out by trial-and-error, of course, a long time ago.

It's a lousy detail and the best types don't generally end up there; most of us didn't have a connection of any sort, or we wouldn't have been on the post in the first place. In my case, they were out to nail me for that mess on Deneb X years ago, where they still think I was responsible for the survey missing the uranium deposits. There's no truth in that at all, but they've been after me ever since.

The only saving grace of the assignment is the natives. Friendly little beasts; stupid as hell, of course, and almost ineducable, but cooperative. They can learn the language after a fashion, and they can be taught to perform simple tasks, but I do not believe that this in itself indicates human intelligence. Too, they look like asses, and it may just be my xenophobia, but nothing that looks like an ass can earn my respect.

But they're pleasant creatures, they make ideal pets, and even a man in the heaviest gear can ride on them for hours. They have an amazing tolerance and they're curious as hell in the bargain, so one way or the other I guess that you could say that it is possible to establish some kind of a relationship with them. I don't want to get into this business of telepathy at all; I know that it's being discussed here, along with all those other mysterious powers they're supposed to have. I never saw any evidence of it, and I should know. And the whole history of the survey, which I know as well as anyone, shows that there's never been any trouble between them and us. They just function on their own level.

I heard about the idea of the pageant only when it was presented to me by a group of the men. Hawkins, one of the botany detail, was the spokesman, more or less, which I found surprising because Hawkins has always struck me as a kind of nonentity, one of those civil servants who make up the bulk of these teams, doing their jobs with all the efficiency and imagination they might possess if they were working in a huge bureau back here. I suppose certain things are timeless after all, but Hawkins was really enthused. I had never seen so much life in the man.

"We want to have a Christmas pageant," he said. "We can build a crèche right outside, and the men will take the various roles, and the Rigellians can be the donkeys in the manger and the sheep on the fields. The idea is to reenact the Nativity and give us all something to think about in our pasts or back home. We want your permission to go ahead and build the crèche."

"I don't understand," I said, which I truly didn't. "Do you mean to say that you're going to assign the various roles of the story to people in the crew and just go through with this thing outside, in that terrain?"

"Exactly. We all kind of worked it out on our own, the engineers and the science detail. We think something should be done for Christmas. We didn't always live out here, you know."

"But what's the point? Why all the enthusiasm?" and indeed, Hawkins and the others were trembling with interest; I had never seen the men so involved. "And what's the point of it?"

"It's kind of a tribute to our history. To what we are as men and where we used to be and what we once wanted to believe and where we are going. It's a reconstitution of myth within a contemporary framework, an infusion of dreams into the reality so that in the blending the two, dreams and reality, must be known together."

"That's a strange way to talk," I said. "I don't believe I've ever heard you talk like that before."

"We kind of worked it out beforehand," Hawkins said and looked at the floor. "Is it all right? Can we go ahead and do it then?"

"I don't even know if you need my permission. This would come under recreation which you are permitted on your respective schedules. I suppose it would take place inside the project?"

"Well, no. We wanted to go outside. There's a nice depression, only a few hundred yards from here where the crèche can be set up, and we kind of thought that it should be in the open air. I can't explain why, but it seemed nicer that way."

"And these roles? You've already selected the people to play them? Won't there be some embarrassment about—uh—some of the assignments?"

"I'm going to play the Infant," Hawkins said. "And the others will fall into place." He pointed to the three who had come with him. "They're going to be the wise men, of course."

Of course. Well, I had no objection. I told him so. It wasn't my place to comment on it one way or the other; a commander's duties are very strictly outlined under the general code, and they do not involve intermingling with the crew on projects or recreation of their own choice which does not interfere with duty.

The idea struck me as being a little strange, of course, immature and a bit preposterous, but as far as I was concerned, that was none of my business.

"You can have your pageant," I said. "I wouldn't advise abusing the natives, though, in the performance."

"Oh, not at all," Hawkins said. "They're kind of the key to the whole thing. The pastoral element and so on. We'll treat them very carefully. Actually, they're quite excited about the idea. It will enable them to know us better."

That's as far as I went with it. It sounded a little crazy, of course, but men tend to get crazy on these expeditions anyway; it's a kind of fringe benefit. I know some who have invented variations of chess and others who have papered their barracks, ceiling to floor, wall to wall, with pictures of various anatomical parts; I know more than a couple who progressed from serious alcoholism to madness during a run. This is what is going to happen inevitably when you set out to colonize the universe: men have to do it, men have to occupy it, and men are going to bring what they are along with them. The idea of having a pageant was no more insane than my conviction, during my second tour of duty on Campa I, that I was regressing to an apelike state due to boredom and would be able to write the first logical autobiography of a subhuman species. You have to go along with this kind of thing.

When I learned that Hawkins had bowed out and Cullings had stepped in, it was of no interest to me; and when I was invited and went, it was only a way of showing the men respect and killing a couple of hours. I didn't like what happened, of course, and in a general human way I feel kind of responsible, but there was no way that we could know. How could anybody know? Besides, in the long run, it probably won't make any difference anyway. Cullings, I understand from people who knew him, was a sullen, non-religious type; maybe the experience will do him some good. On the other hand, I don't like this kind of inquiry, and I have nothing more to say.

STOCK, PSYCHOLOGIST: There is a perfectly rational explanation for what happened, but you will not obtain it from many of the others, particularly not from Williams, whom I diagnosed early on as a rigid, repressed, anal-oriented paranoid whose fantasies were an enactment and rationalization of his basic, latent homosexuality. Of course, my job is to deal more with alien psychology and social relationships, but that doesn't prevent me from making judgments.

You have to do something to keep the intellect alive, after all: these aliens—most of those I've encountered and particularly the bastards on the Rigel survey— are little better than vegetables, and there's hardly much stimulation in working out group patterns and social interaction on a survey team because anybody who's on these is half-crazy in the first place and then they proceed to get crazier. By the time I got wind of the pageant and the way it was going, it was my best opinion that Cullings, Hawkins and the whole batch of them had regressed to a subinfantile state where they were using magic and mysticism as a way of warding off any kind of threat; they were even below the polymorphous perverse stage. I could catch that right away by the peculiar details of the pageant which they insisted upon—the relationship of the Madonna and child in the feeding position, the way that the aliens were grouped just around, the use of special straw for the crèche . . . all of this was sheer compulsiveness. And the fact that a big, hulking man like Forrest was playing the role of the Madonna with little Cullings added another element to it. The implications were fascinating; it was the first truly interesting thing that had happened to me since I signed up for this cursed project. But then again it could get a thoughtful man scared.

Several things scared me: in the first place, as I began to make my investigations, then quietly checking here and there, I found that nobody would really own up to having originated the idea of the pageant. "It just kind of came up one day and we got to work on it" was what I heard time and again, or "a lot of us just realized that it would be a honey of an idea." The sudden imposition of a mass-obsession without clear, individual origin is one of the surest indications that something is going on. I didn't like it.

I'm aware that it's been brought up now that the idea might have originated with the aliens who were using their telepathic ability to plant it in the crew so subtly that the crew thought it came out of their own heads. It would be a good explanation, but it doesn't make a pack of sense: these aliens are idiots in every possible regard; they are animalic not only in appearance but in behavior, and the fact that they have a low mimetic ability and are thus able to simulate language is no clue whatsoever to intelligence. No, the men got this up on their very own—mass-psychosis if it ever happened—and what happened to Cullings was totally their responsibility.

When you take a group of hacks, boobs, oafs and civil servants, set them up on a bleak outpost somewhere near the center of hell—otherwise to be known as the outer arm of the Milky Way—leave them to their own devices sans sex, sans organized recreation, sans the inner resources to make things come out their own way, and when this group of men ends up raving religious fanatics who perform a strange rite out of which comes death, disappearance and madness . . . what other explanation do you need? It is not so much that I am an excessively rational man . . . but after all, how far afield does one have to go? The simplest explanation is the right one; I learned that a long time ago. The simplest explanation is the right one here. I will not cooperate with this inquiry any further, and I care little what happens to me as a result of it.

MARTINSON, CREW: Well, I'll give you a simple account, as best as I can remember. I don't know why you're asking me; all those other guys who testified would be much better able to do it than me. I'm just a simple athlete. Haven't you heard? I'll just stick to the facts. The rehearsals went pretty well, although the time when Cullings and Hawkins switched roles set us back a little. The whole point was not to make a mockery of it. I was playing one of the people in the inn; I had only one line which was after the innkeeper said no room I was supposed to get up and say "But what of the child?" Just that, "But what of the child?" It was the key to the whole scene, but there was so much else going on that nobody listened.

The aliens worked into it just great. They not only played the animals, there were plenty left over to be in the tavern as well. There was nothing peculiar about them playing human roles; we just took it for granted. They really worked into it and they were good actors, too.

So, the night we did it, it went just like the rehearsals, all the way up to the end, when things changed a little. What we were supposed to do, as I recall, was simply to group around Cullings and look at him, and then the floodlights that we had set up would be switched off, and that would be the end of the thing. Cullings looked very peaceful; he took the role seriously. All during rehearsals, as soon as he stepped in, he was saying that he felt for the first time as if he had truly discovered himself. Recovered himself? Maybe; I forget.

But when the lights were supposed to go on out, they didn't. I have no idea what happened; maybe somebody at the controls wasn't there. Anyway, the lights just kept on glaring and there were the whole bunch of us, standing on the straw, most of us in robes and some of us sitting up on the Rigellians.

The words? Yeah. You want to know those. I don't know who it came from, one of the donkeys, maybe mine, maybe another, and they said Thou Art My Own Beloved Son; I beckon unto thee and we art conjoined forever. That was all. The voice sounded pleased.

Cullings . . . he began to shake.

He shook and shook and then he was drooling and slobbering and crying. It wasn't like the rehearsals at all; it was as if he was having a fit or something, and he began to scream things like "I see, I see" and "What is going on here?" and "The thieves, they double-crossed me!" and it didn't sound like his voice at all, it was so strained and high-pitched. Then he started to throw himself around on the straw. Like epilepsy. Only more interesting.

The whole bunch of us were just so stunned that we didn't even go in to pick him up or try to help him. We just stared. It was kind of frightening because we hadn't counted on it, you see; we were just going to shut off the lights and go back to the ship and have a few drinks. And sing the old carols. All of a sudden, we have a situation. He was twitching and jerking like mad, Cullings; it was like he was trying to stand up but he simply couldn't make it. He would get to his knees and then it would happen again.

And then, of course, he said those words.

Well, of course, I was upset. Cullings wasn't exactly a close friend, but I knew him and when you live in close quarters with a guy, you tend to get involved. I was very sorry to see what had happened to him, but there just wasn't a damned thing I could do. There wasn't a damned thing anyone could do; we just stood there like a pack of fools. And the asses. After a while, when we realized that it was over and yet it wasn't going to stop, someone said that we might as well get back to the ship and have a few drinks anyway. Nobody wanted to touch Cullings, although someone suggested we drag him over there. We just couldn't bear to. So we left him there surrounded by the donkeys and we went back. Midway into the ship we saw the floodlights get cut, and then we went inside and got really stoned. All that I know is that Captain Williams said we should all leave the planet immediately, and that was some operation, you can imagine, with over half of us staggering drunk, trying to work on the ship. But we got it off, and we got back here in

good shape, and then all of a sudden we found ourselves with this court of inquiry and like that. I don't
know what's going on. I have great sympathy for Cullings, though. I sometimes think about what he must
be doing now. If anything. But I try not to think about
these things at all.

PETERS, FIRST SECRETARY: I think that the
evidence, based upon what we have heard and upon
the "statement" of the alien, is pretty conclusive. In-
cidentally, that alien is going to die if we don't get
him back there soon. We cannot simulate their environment; there are things about it we don't understand.

It is really conclusive, and I don't think there's much
point in going on further. Our decision to make is
simple: do we go back to Rigel XIV or don't we? Since
I can see no basis for our returning other than to
reenact a continuing madness, I think we should stay
out.

I think we should stay out of a lot of places, I really
do. There are forces in this universe which we are not
meant to understand, and our attempts to make them
conform to our vision of rationality can only make us
cosmic clowns to far more than the Rigellians if we
keep this up. I think that the Bureau will carefully
have to review all of its procedures and policies now
and that we are in for a period of regrouping and
terrible reappraisal.

As for what may happen in the decades to come,
this is something that we cannot possibly ascertain.
Whatever happens, it is something that we will have
to live with. I can only trust that religiosity for them,
as it was for us, proves to be a localized phenomenon.

And I call upon the mercy of this court; I do not think that charges should be filed against the deponents. What did they know? What do we know? In similar circumstances, we would have done the same. We are that kind of people. Give them desk jobs and let them alone.

We cannot make a Civil Service adjunct of the universe. I think that this, at least, is pretty clear.

LAST WORDS OF CULLINGS, ABSENT: *My God, my God, 32 years to go —*
  But I'd rather be getting crocked at the Inn!

Christmas Roses

John Christopher

The skipper cushioned us in nicely. I had my eyes on the dial the whole time and the needle never got above four and a half G's. With a boat like the *Arkland* that was good; I've known a bad pilot touch seven G's on an Earth landing. All the same, I didn't feel so hot. Young Stenway was out of his cradle before the tremors had stopped. I lay still a moment while he stood over me, grinning.

He said: "Break it up, Joe. Dreaming of a pension?"

I got up with a bounce and landed him a playful clip that rocked him back into his own cradle. There was normal gravity underneath us; the feeling of rightness you know in your bones and muscles no matter how long you've been away. It was good to feel myself tough still.

Stenway said: "So this is Washington. What day is it?"

I said: "You revert to type quick, kid. How should I know what day it is? I'm only a visitor."

He grinned, flushing a little, and went over to the multiple calendar. I saw him fingering it, his face screwed up.

He said: "Friday. Say, Joe. If we take more than fourteen days on the turn-round we'll make Christmas here."

I said: "If we take more than ten days on the turn-round the whole Board of Directors will commit gory suicide. What's worrying you? You'll get plum duff in Luna City."

He grinned lopsidedly and went out in a hurry. I was a bit sorry for him. He'd done less than a year in the service. Things weren't the right pattern for him yet. He probably thought some of us were tough eggs. But we had to ride him down now and then for his own good.

I went along to see Louie. He'd been in space only a couple of years less than I had, and we'd both been with the *Arkland* since she was commissioned eight years before. But we didn't see each other much, working on different shifts and pretty nearly at opposite ends of the boat. I found him in the mess, sprucing up.

He said: "Hello, Joe. You still with us?"

I said: "Why not? I'm only young once."

"Borrowed time," he said. "Just borrowed time."

I said: "Louie. Do me a favour."

He said: "Any little thing."

He put down a hairbrush and started powdering his face, overlaying the finely ravelled seams of red that told he'd been out in vacuum. I couldn't understand that myself. It made you a bit unusual on Earth, it stamped you as a spaceman—but, hell, who'd be ashamed of that? Still, I've never been branded myself, so maybe I shouldn't talk.

I said: "You're handling the loading for the next trip?"

He pressed the powder in with his finger-tips, and nodded.

"I want to get something on board," I said.

"How big?" he asked.

I shrugged lightly. "About five feet long. Maybe three feet across each way, at its widest. But it will squeeze a bit."

Louie jutted his chin out and flicked a patch of black velvet across his face. He spoke through his teeth.

"What about the Pentagon building, if you want a souvenir?"

I said: "What would I do with the Pentagon building?"

Louie turned around.

"Look, Joe, you know how things are. You know the cost of space-freighting. There isn't a quarter-ounce of cargo-weight that isn't accounted for. What do you want to fit in, anyway?"

"It's for old Hans," I told him. "I thought of taking him a Christmas-tree."

Louie didn't say anything for a moment. He had brushed the powder well in, but you could still see the crimson network underneath. At last he said:

"O.K. Get it up here the night before we blast. I'll fix it for you."

I said: "Thanks, Louie. When will that be, by the way? Have they told you?"

"Nineteenth," he said. "Now go and raise hell for nine days. Don't forget the medical tomorrow."

I looked at him sharply, but he was brushing another layer of powder in. Medical was a routine, always taken between eighteen and twenty-four hours after cushioning. The doctors knew why, or said they did. It wasn't the sort of thing you needed to be reminded of. But it wasn't worth taking him up on it.

The *Arkland* touched at Washington every fifth trip. I knew quite a few numbers and I went all out to raise my usual cain. There was a sombre moment once when one of the girls relaxed and the wrinkles stood out, but it passed. There's always the younger generation. I let it get round to two days from blasting before I dropped in on the company's office. They've got a block of masonry on Roosevelt Boulevard that's bigger than Luna City. Welfare is on Floor 32. It makes me airsick to look out of their windows.

There was a little blonde at the desk. She said hello very brightly. It occurred to me that next time I might contact Welfare at the beginning of a furlough. She looked as though she could get through my back-pay as well as any.

I said: "You can help me out. I want to buy something."

She was restrained but eager.

I said: "Yeah. I want to buy a Christmas-tree."

She looked surprised and rather disappointed, but she was business-like. She waded through a pile of directories like a terrier after rats.

"Christmas-trees," she said. "Your best bet is the Leecliff Nurseries. Mr. Cliff. About fifteen miles out. You can pick up a gyro on the roof."

I said: "Don't tell me there's a roof on this thing."

She smiled very nicely.

I said: "Keep a week free next November. I'll be back."

The gyro did the trip in just over ten minutes. Where it put me down you wouldn't guess such a place as Washington existed. One way there were a lot of low sheds and a few glass-houses. The other way there were just fields and fields of plants growing. I realised that it was more than ten years since I'd been outside a city on an Earth furlough. You get into habits. It occurred to me that I might have been missing something.

They had phoned Mr. Cliff I was coming; "Good Service" is the company's motto. He was waiting when the gyro touched. A little round fellow, with a look as though something had surprised him. He said:

"Major Davies, I'm delighted to see you. We don't see many spacemen out here. Come and see my roses."

He seemed eager and I let him take me. I wasn't breaking my neck to get back into town.

He had a glass-house full of roses. I hesitated in the doorway. Mr. Cliff said: "Well?"

"I'd forgotten they smelled like that," I said.

He said proudly: "It's quite a showing. A week before Christmas and a showing like that. Look at this Frau Karl Druschki."

It was a white rose, very nicely shaped and scented like spring. The roses had me. I crawled round after Mr. Cliff, seeing roses, feeling roses, breathing roses. I looked at my watch when it began to get dark.

I said: "I came to buy a Christmas-tree."

We left the rose-house reluctantly. Mr. Cliff said: "Christmas on Earth for a change?"

I liked Mr. Cliff. I said:

"No—Luna City. It's for someone there."

He waited for me to go on.

"A guy called Hans," I said. "He's been nearly forty years in Luna City. He was born in a little village in Austria. Halfway up a mountain, with pines all round and snow on them in winter. You know. He gets homesick."

Mr. Cliff said: "Why doesn't he come back?"

It's always a shock when people show how little they know about the life you lead, though I suppose you can't blame them.

I said to Mr. Cliff: "The doctors have it all tabbed. It's what they call cumulative stress. You can't bring a boat in or push her off without an initial strain. It varies with the planets, of course. For Earth, with an average-sized vessel, the peak's about five or six gravities."

I flexed my shoulders back, breathing this different air.

"You've got to be tough physically," I said. "But, even so, it tells. It's the heart chiefly. They give you a warning when it begins to flicker; you can drop out then with a pension. Of course, there are some who can carry on. They're used to the life, and ..."

"And ...?" said Mr. Cliff.

"There's a final warning as well. They check up on you after each trip; vet you for the next. Then one time it's just a plain No. You can argue, but the answer's No. Another take-off would finish you. So they say. There's no way of testing it; they just don't let you on a boat after that."

Mr. Cliff said: "They're very considerate."

I laughed. "Oh, very. The only thing is—they check you each landfall. Hans got his final warning at Luna City."

Mr. Cliff said: "Oh." He bent his head to smell the red rose in his coat. "How long ago did you say?"

"Hans is an old man. Over seventy. Generally you get your first warning when you're about thirty. Near enough forty years, I suppose."

"And how big is this Luna City?"

"That's easy," I said. "It's in the guide books. A couple of blocks long by a block wide. It goes underground a bit as well."

"That's terrible," Mr. Cliff said softly. "Forty years like that. No trees, no birds. . . . And young men know that and still take the risk? I can't believe it."

It was an old story, but I'd never felt myself getting so mad about it before. I reined myself in. He was a nice old guy.

I said: "You don't understand, Mr. Cliff. There's something in the life. And sometimes there's more than five years between first and final warnings. One guy went ten. There's always one more trip that's worth making before you settle down for good. They don't recruit spacemen who give up easily. And you may always strike lucky and get your ticket at this end."

He said gently: "When did you get your first warning, Major Davies?"

I flushed. "Three years ago. So what? Now this matter of the Christmas-tree, Mr. Cliff. . . ."

Mr. Cliff said: "I'll show you. The Christmas-tree is on me. Please. I want to."

I said: "Thanks, Mr. Cliff. For Hans, too."

"I own some stock in Lunar Mines." He blinked. "Forty years. . . ."

He led me away to show me the fir trees, and the scent of roses gave way to a rich piney smell that made me remember being a kid, and holidays up in the lakes. He said:

"I've been thinking, Major Davies. I've got a proposition that may interest you. . . ."

I didn't see Louie when the tree went on board; one of his boys handled it. There wasn't a sign of any of the company police around, and I guessed Louie was distracting them down at the night-office in a friendly game of poker. Skinning 'em, too, if I knew Louie. I didn't see him until the end of my second shift on the trip. The radar screen was a beautiful blank; it was a clear season for meteors. Louie was lolling in front of it reading *The Three Musketeers*.

I said: "I always knew I slipped up when I majored in Nav. Do they pay you for this?"

Sometimes there's ill feeling about the large stretches of easy time radar-ops manage to corner, but Louie knew I'd been in space too long for that. Until the automatic relays smarten up a lot there's got to be a man on the screen. And the company doesn't give time away; the radar section handle the quarter-mastering, too. Every third furlough they lose two days.

Louie grinned. "I've got a weak heart. Didn't you know?"

I tossed him a cigarette. "Thanks for getting baby on board. What did you throw out—gold bars?"

He shook his head. "Just my own brand of math. If that orbit you've laid us turns out bad enough we'll hit the sun approximately ten minutes sooner than we would otherwise. And I've got to pep my meteor deflection up by three thousandths of a second. It's a big risk."

"My orbit's good," I said. "I'll only ever lay one better. Next trip I'm going to lay the tightest Moon-Earth orbit since Christiansen came in on the Leonids. After that you needn't worry about my failing eyes, Louie."

He said: "I'm glad, Joe. I always knew you had sense. I'm dropping out the moment they give me a hint. It's not worth it."

I said: "Yes. I'm really going."

Louie said: "You'll miss it, but you'll get over that. You would have to, anyway, before long."

I said: "It's out in the country, Louie. A nursery. Growing plants, all kinds of plants. Fir trees and chrysanthemums and daffodils—and roses at Christmas. And the moon's no more than something you plant by. I shan't miss anything."

He said: "You're lucky, Joe. That's what it is—you're lucky."

We cushioned at three G's and I felt it again; a long ache inside my chest as though my heart and lungs were tied up with strings and someone was twisting them nice and slowly. It was all right after a few minutes, and I got up, light and active under Moon gravity. I wasted no time getting through the main lock. I looked for old Hans amongst those who stood by, but there was no sign of him. I called Portugese, who runs the grog shop.

"Portugese! Where's Hans? I've got something for him."

He came waddling over airily. With a bulk like his I could almost understand why he had chosen Luna City. He shrugged, lifting everything: hands, shoulders and eyebrows.

"Too late now," he said. "He died just after nightfall. We're taking him out in a few hours."

*   *   *

In Luna City there are no extras. You don't waste
anything that has to be freighted a quarter of a million miles, and that includes oxygen. When men die
there, their bodies are kept until nightfall, when, for
three hundred and thirty-six hours, darkness freezes
into rime the last traces of the Moon's atmosphere.
Some time during the night the body is taken out in
a Caterpillar and committed, with duly economical
rites, to some cleft in the antique rocks. With the
sunrise the thin air melts, the grey lichen runs like a
sickness along the crater bottoms, and in that jungle
the minute lunar insects awaken to fight battles as
real as Tyrannosaurus ever knew. Long before the
crater shadows lengthen towards sunset the cleft is
empty again. No flesh, no hair, no scrap of bone es-
capes them.

Portugese drove the Caterpillar out through the air-
lock. Louie and I sat behind him with old Hans' body,
covered by a sheet, on the floor between us. We were
silent while the little truck jolted on its metal tracks
across granite and pumice and frozen lava. And I
don't think it was the death inside that silenced us;
we had liked old Hans, but he had had his time, and
was released now to infinity from the narrow confines
of Luna City. It was the death outside that quietened
us, as it quietens any man who goes out among those
age-old crests and pinnacles, under those glaring
stars.

Portugese halted the Caterpillar on the crest of a
rise about mid-way between Luna City and Kelly's
Crater. It was the usual burial ground; the planet's
surface here was cross-hatched in deep grooves by
some age-old catastrophe. We clamped down the vi-

sors on our suits and got out. Portugese and I carried old Hans easily between us, his frail body fantastically light against lunar gravity. We put him down carefully in a wide, deep cleft, and I turned round towards the truck. Louie walked towards us, carrying the Christmas-tree. There had been moisture on it which had frozen instantly into sparkling frost. It looked like a centre-piece out of a store shop window. It had seemed a good idea back in Luna City, but now it didn't seem appropriate.

We wedged it in with rocks, Portugese read a prayer, and we walked back to the Caterpillar, glad to be able to let our visors down again and light up cigarettes. We stayed there while we smoked, looking through the front screen. The tree stood up green and white against the sullen, hunching blackness of Kelly's Crater. Right overhead was the Earth, glowing with daylight. I could make out Italy, clear and unsmudged, but further north Hans' beloved Austria was hidden under blotching December cloud.

We didn't say anything. Portugese squeezed out his cigarette and started the Caterpillar up, turning her round again towards Luna City. We ran into B lock, and Portugese stabled the truck and came out again to join us. He put his fat arms around our shoulders.

"Come on, boys. Always a drink on the house after a burying party."

Louie said: "Medical first, Portugese. We'll look in afterwards. Keep the rum hot for us."

We saw him glide plumply away, and turned back ourselves towards the Admin. buildings. The others had been through the Medical while we were out, and we had a doctor each without any waiting. We sat in the anteroom afterwards, waiting for them to write our cards up before we could collect them. At last the call came through on the speaker:

"Major Graves. Squadron Enderby. Cards ready now."

Louie got his first. He looked at the big blue stamp on the front—FIRST WARNING. He grinned.

"We'll go out in harness, Joe. Any chance of a third partnership in that flower business?"

I didn't say anything. I could see my card before the doctor gave it to me. I saw the red star splashed on it, and I'd seen too many of them not to know what it meant. It was the mark of the exile, the outlaw who had left it too late to get back. It was the beginning of such a story as the one whose end, forty years later, I had witnessed in the lee of Kelly's Crater under the mocking globe of Earth.

I said: "This is my last trip, Doc. When we hit Antwerp I'm retiring."

He shook his head. "I'm sorry, Major."

I said: "I don't care if it's a million to one chance, Doc. I'll take it; and no hard feelings if it doesn't come off. I'll sign any disclaimer the company wants."

He said: "It's no good, Major. You know the regulations. These things are too fool-proof now. We're not allowed to let you commit suicide."

I knew it was no good, too. Louie had gone. We all knew better than to stick around when someone got the red star. I had time to look at the doctor. He was very young and didn't look very happy. I guessed he hadn't handed out a star before.

He said: "It could be worse, Major. It could have been Phobos."

I looked at him and he looked away. I walked out slowly.

* * *

From the top level in Luna City you can see the sky; at night the stars and the softly glowing Earth. Down to the west Sirius blazes over Kelly's Crater. I've been up here for hours watching them.

I keep thinking I can smell roses.

Happy Birthday, Dear Jesus

Frederik Pohl

It was the craziest Christmas I ever spent. Partly it was Heinemann's fault—he came up with a new wrinkle in gift-wrapping that looked good but like every other idea that comes out of the front office meant plenty of headaches for the rest of us. But what really messed up Christmas for me was the girl.

Personnel sent her down—after I'd gone up there myself three times and banged my fist on the table. It was the height of the season and when she told me that she had had her application in *three weeks* before they called her, I excused myself and got Personnel on the store phone from my private office. "Martin here," I said. "What the devil's the matter with you people? This girl is the Emporium type if I ever saw one, and you've been letting her sit around nearly a month while—"

Crawford, the Personnel head, interrupted me.

"Have you talked to her very much?" he wanted to know.

"Well, no. But—"

"Call me back when you do," he advised, and clicked off.

I went back to the stockroom where she was standing patiently, and looked her over a little thoughtfully. But she looked all right to me. She was blond-haired and blue-eyed and not very big; she had a sweet, slow smile. She wasn't exactly beautiful, but she looked like a girl you'd want to know. She wasn't bold, and she wasn't too shy; and that's a perfect description of what we call "The Emporium Type."

So what in the world was the matter with Personnel?

Her name was Lilymary Hargreave. I put her to work on the gift-wrap spraying machine while I got busy with my paper work. I have a hundred forty-one persons in the department and at the height of the Christmas season I could use twice as many. But we do get the work done. For instance, Saul & Capell, the next biggest store in town, has a hundred and sixty in their gift and counseling department, and their sales run easily twenty-five per cent less than ours. And in the four years that I've headed the department we've yet to fail to get an order delivered when it was promised.

All through that morning I kept getting glimpses of the new girl. She was a quick learner—smart, too smart to be stuck with the sprayer for very long. I needed someone like her around, and right there on the spot I made up my mind that if she was as good as she looked I'd put her in a counseling booth within a week, and the devil with what Personnel thought.

The store was packed with last-minute shoppers. I suppose I'm sentimental, but I love to watch the thousands of people bustling in and out, with all the displays going at once, and the lights on the trees, and the loudspeakers playing *White Christmas* and *The Eighth Candle* and *Jingle Bells* and all the other traditional old favorites. Christmas is more than a mere selling season of the year to me; it *means* something.

The girl called me over near closing time. She looked distressed and with some reason. There was a dolly filled with gift-wrapped packages, and a man from Shipping looking annoyed. She said, "I'm sorry, Mr. Martin, but I seem to have done something wrong."

The Shipping man snorted. "Look for yourself, Mr. Martin," he said, handing me one of the packages.

I looked. It was wrong, all right. Heinemann's new wrinkle that year was a special attached gift card—a simple Yule scene and the printed message:

The very Merriest of Season's Greetings

From.....

To.......

$8.50

The price varied with the item, of course. Heinemann's idea was for the customer to fill it out and mail it, ahead of time, to the person it was intended for. That way, the person who got it would know just about how much he ought to spend on a present for the first person. It was smart, I admit, and maybe the smartest thing about it was rounding the price off to the nearest fifty cents instead of giving it exactly. Heinemann said it was bad-mannered to be too precise—and the way the customers were going for the idea, it had to be right.

But the trouble was that the gift-wrapping machines were geared to only a plain card; it was necessary for the operator to put the price in by hand.

I said, "That's all right, Joe; I'll take care of it." As Joe went satisfied back to Shipping, I told the girl: "It's my fault. I should have explained to you, but I guess I've just been a little too rushed."

She looked downcast. "I'm sorry," she said.

"Nothing to be sorry about." I showed her the routing slip attached to each one, which the Shipping Department kept for its records once the package was on its way. "All we have to do is go through these; the price is on every one. We'll just fill out the cards and get them out. I guess—" I looked at my watch— "I guess you'll be a little late tonight, but I'll see that you get overtime and dinner money for it. It wasn't your mistake, after all."

She said hesitantly, "Mr. Martin, couldn't it—well, can I let it go for tonight? It isn't that I mind working, but I keep house for my father and if I don't get there on time he just won't remember to eat dinner. Please?"

I suppose I frowned a little, because her expression was a little worried. But, after all, it was her first day. I said, "Miss Hargreave, don't give it a thought. I'll take care of it."

The way I took care of it, it turned out, was to do it myself; it was late when I got through, and I ate quickly and went home to bed. But I didn't mind, for oh! the sweetness of the smile she gave me as she left.

I looked forward to the next morning, because I was looking forward to seeing Lilymary Hargreave again. But my luck was out—for she was.

My number-two man, Johnny Furness, reported that she hadn't phoned either. I called Personnel to get her phone number, but they didn't have it; I got the address, but the phone company had no phone listed under her name. So I stewed around until the coffee break, and then I put my hat on and headed out of the store. It wasn't merely that I was interested in seeing her, I told myself; she was just too good a worker to get off on the wrong foot this way, and it was only simple justice for me to go to her home and set her straight.

Her house was in a nondescript neighborhood—not too good, not too bad. A gang of kids were playing under a fire hydrant at the corner—but, on the other hand, the houses were neat and nearly new. Middle-class, you'd have to say.

I found the address, and knocked on the door of a second-floor apartment.

It was opened by a tall, leathery man of fifty or so—Lilymary's father, I judged. "Good morning," I said. "Is Miss Hargreave at home?"

He smiled; his teeth were bright in a very sun-bronzed face. "Which one?"

"Blond girl, medium height, blue eyes. Is there more than one?"

"There are four. But you mean Lilymary; won't you come in?"

I followed him, and a six-year-old edition of Lilymary took my hat and gravely hung it on a rack made of bamboo pegs. The leathery man said, "I'm Morton Hargreave, Lily's father. She's in the kitchen."

"George Martin," I said. He nodded and left me, for the kitchen, I presumed. I sat down on an old-fashioned studio couch in the living room, and the six-year-old sat on the edge of a straight-backed chair across from me, making sure I didn't pocket any of the souvenirs on the mantel. The room was full of curiosities—what looked like a cloth of beaten bark hanging on one wall, with a throwing-spear slung over the cloth. Everything looked vaguely South-Seas, though I am no expert.

The six-year-old said seriously, "This is the man, Lilymary," and I got up.

"Good morning," said Lilymary Hargreave, with a smudge of flour and an expression of concern on her face.

I said, floundering, "I, uh, noticed you hadn't come in and, well, since you were new to the Emporium, I thought—"

"I *am* sorry, Mr. Martin," she said. "Didn't Personnel tell you about Sundays?"

"What about Sundays?"

"I must have my Sundays off," she explained. "Mr. Crawford said it was very unusual, but I really can't accept the job any other way."

"Sundays off?" I repeated. "But—but, Miss Hargreave, don't you see what that does to my schedule? Sunday's our busiest day! The Emporium isn't a rich man's shop; our customers work during the week. If we aren't staffed to serve them when they can come in, we just aren't doing the job they expect of us!"

She said sincerely, "I'm terribly sorry, Mr. Martin."

The six-year-old was already reaching for my hat. From the doorway her father said heartily, "Come back again, Mr. Martin. We'll be glad to see you."

He escorted me to the door, as Lilymary smiled and nodded and headed back to the kitchen. I said, "Mr.

Hargreave, won't you ask Lilymary to come in for the afternoon, at least? I hate to sound like a boss, but I'm really short-handed on weekends, right now at the peak of the season."

"Season?"

"The Christmas season," I explained. "Nearly ninety per cent of our annual business is done in the Christmas season, and a good half of it on weekends. So won't you ask her?"

He shook his head. "Six days the Lord labored, Mr. Martin," he boomed, "and the seventh was the day of rest. I'm sorry."

And there I was, outside the apartment and the door closing politely but implacably behind me.

Crazy people. I rode the subway back to the store in an irritable mood; I bought a paper, but I didn't read it, because every time I looked at it all I saw was the date that showed me how far the Christmas season already had advanced, how little time we had left to make our quotas and beat last year's record: the eighth of September.

I would have something to say to Miss Lilymary Hargreave when she had the kindness to show up at her job. I promised myself. But, as it turned out, I didn't. Because that night, checking through the day's manifolds when everyone else had gone home, I fell in love with Lilymary Hargreave.

Possibly that sounds silly to you. She wasn't even there, and I'd only known her for a few hours, and when a man begins to push thirty without ever being married, you begin to think he's a hard case and not likely to fall slambang, impetuously in love like a teen-ager after his first divorce. But it's true, all the same.

I almost called her up. I trembled on the brink of it, with my hand on the phone. But it was close to midnight, and if she wasn't home getting ready for bed I didn't want to know it, so I went home to my own bed. I reached under the pillow and turned off my dreamster before I went to sleep; I had a full library for it, a de luxe model with five hundred dreams that had been a present from the firm the Christmas before. I had Haroun al Rashid's harem and three of Charles Second's favorites on tape, and I had rocketing around the moon and diving to Atlantis and winning a sweepstakes and getting elected king of the world; but what I wanted to dream about was not on anybody's tape, and its name was Lilymary Hargreave.

Monday lasted forever. But at the end of forever, when the tip of the nightingale's wing had brushed away the mountain of steel and the Shipping personnel were putting on their hats and coats and powdering their noses or combing their hair, I stepped right up to Lilymary Hargreave and asked her to go to dinner with me.

She looked astonished, but only for a moment. Then she smiled. . . . I have mentioned the sweetness of her smile. "It's wonderful of you to ask me, Mr. Martin," she said earnestly, "and I do appreciate it. But I can't."

"Please," I said.

"I *am* sorry."

I might have said please again, and I might have fallen to my knees at her feet, it was that important to me. But the staff was still in the shop, and how would it look for the head of the department to fall at the feet of his newest employee? I said woodenly, "That's too bad." And I nodded and turned away, leaving her frowning after me. I cleared my desk sloppily, chucking the invoices in a drawer, and I was halfway out the door when I heard her calling after me:

"Mr. Martin, Mr. Martin!"

She was hurrying toward me, breathless. "I'm sorry," she said, "I didn't mean to scream at you. But I just phoned my father, and—"

"I thought you didn't have a phone," I said accusingly.

She blinked at me. "At the rectory," she explained. "Anyway, I just phoned him, and—well, we'd both be delighted if you would come and have dinner with us at home."

Wonderful words! The whole complexion of the shipping room changed in a moment. I beamed foolishly at her, with a soft surge at my heart; I felt happy enough to endow a home, strong enough to kill a cave bear or give up smoking or any crazy, mixed-up thing. I wanted to shout and sing; but all I said was: "That sounds great." We headed for the subway, and although I must have talked to her on the ride I cannot remember a word we said, only that she looked like the angel at the top of our tallest Christmas tree.

Dinner was good, and there was plenty of it, cooked by Lilymary herself, and I think I must have seemed a perfect idiot. I sat there, with the six-year-old on one side of me and Lilymary on the other, across from the ten-year-old and the twelve-year-old. The father of them all was at the head of the table, but he was the only other male. I understood there were a couple

of brothers, but they didn't live with the others. I
suppose there had been a mother at some time, unless
Morton Hargreave stamped the girls out with a kind
of cookie-cutter; but whatever she had been she appeared to be deceased. I felt overwhelmed. I wasn't
used to being surrounded by young females, particularly as young as the median in that gathering.

Lilymary made an attempt to talk to me, but it
wasn't altogether successful. The younger girls were
given to fits of giggling, which she had to put a stop
to, and to making what were evidently personal remarks in some kind of a peculiar foreign tongue—it
sounded like a weird aboriginal dialect, and I later
found out that it was. But it was disconcerting, especially from the lips of a six-year-old with the giggles.
So I didn't make any very intelligent responses to
Lilymary's overtures.

But all things end, even eating dinner with giggling
girls. And then Mr. Hargreave and I sat in the little
parlor, waiting for the girls to—finish doing the
dishes? I said, shocked, "Mr. Hargreave, do you mean
they *wash* them?"

"Certainly they wash them," he boomed mildly.
"How else would they get them clean, Mr. Martin?"

"Why, *dishwashers*, Mr. Hargreave." I looked at him
in a different way. Business is business. I said, "After
all, this is the Christmas season. At the Emporium we
put a very high emphasis on dishwashers as a Christmas gift, you know. We—"

He interrupted good-humoredly. "I already have
my gifts, Mr. Martin. Four of them, and very fine
dishwashers they are."

"But Mr. Hargreave—"

"Not Mister Hargreave." The six-year-old was

standing beside me, looking disapproving. "*Doctor* Hargreave."

"Corinne!" said her father. "Forgive her, Mr. Martin. But you see we're not very used to the—uh, civilized way of doing things. We've been a long time with the Dyaks."

The girls were all back from the kitchen, and Lilymary was out of her apron and looking—unbelievable. "Entertainment," she said brightly. "Mr. Martin, would you like to hear Corinne play?"

There was a piano in the corner. I said hastily, "I'm crazy about piano music. But—"

Lilymary laughed. "She's good," she told me seriously. "Even if I do have to say it to her face. But we'll let you off that if you like. Gretchen and I sing a little bit, if you'd prefer it?"

Wasn't there any TV in this place? I felt as out of place as an Easterbunny-helper in the Santa Claus line, but Lilymary was still looking unbelievable. So I sat through Lilymary and the twelve-year-old named Gretchen singing ancient songs while the six-year-old named Corinne accompanied them on the piano. It was pretty thick. Then the ten-year-old, whose name I never did catch, did recitations; and then they all looked expectantly at me.

I cleared my throat, slightly embarrassed. Lilymary said quickly, "Oh, you don't have to do anything, Mr. Martin. It's just our custom, but we don't expect strangers to conform to it!"

I didn't want that word "stranger" to stick. I said, "Oh, but I'd like to. I mean, I'm not much good at public entertaining, but—" I hesitated, because that was the truest thing I had ever said. I had no more voice than a goat, and of course the only instrument

I had ever learned to play was a TV set. But then I remembered something from my childhood.

"I'll tell you what," I said enthusiastically. "How would you like something appropriate to the season? 'A Visit from Santa Claus,' for instance?"

Gretchen said snappishly, "What season? *We* don't start celebrating—"

Her father cut her off. "Please do, Mr. Martin," he said politely. "We'd enjoy that very much."

I cleared my throat and started:

> 'Tis the season of Christmas, and all
>   through the house
> St. Nick and his helpers begin their carouse.
> The closets are stuffed and the drawers
>   overflowing
> With gift-wrapped remembrances, coming
>   and going.
> What a joyous abandon of Christmastime
>   glow!
> What a making of lists! What a spending of
>   dough!
> So much for—

"Hey!" said Gretchen, looking revolted. "Daddy, *that* isn't how—"

"Hush!" said Dr. Hargreave grimly. His own expression wasn't very delighted either, but he said, "Please go on."

I began to wish I'd kept my face shut. They were all looking at me very peculiarly, except for Lilymary, who was conscientiously studying the floor. But it was too late to back out; I went on:

So much for the bedroom, so much for the bath,
So much for the kitchen—too little by half!
Come Westinghouse, Philco! Come Hotpoint, G.E.!
Come Sunbeam! Come Mixmaster! Come to the
    Tree!
So much for the wardrobe—how shine Daddy's
    eyes
As he reaps his Yule harvest of slippers and ties.
So much for the family, so much for the friends,
So much for the neighbors—the list never ends.
A contingency fund for the givers belated
Whose gifts must be hastily reciprocated.
And out of—

Gretchen stood up. "It's our bedtime," she said.
"Good night, everybody."

Lilymary flared, "It is not! Now be still!" And she
looked at me for the first time. "Please go on," she
said, with a furrowed brow.

I said hoarsely:

And out of the shops, how they spring with a
    clatter,
The gifts and appliances words cannot flatter!
The robot dishwasher, the new Frigidaire,
The doll with the didy and curlable hair!
The electrified hairbrush, the black lingerie,
The full-color stereoscopic TV!
Come, Credit Department! Come, Personal Loan!
Come, Mortgage, come Christmas Club, come—

Lilymary turned her face away. I stopped and licked
my lips.

"That's all I remember," I lied. "I—I'm sorry if—"

Dr. Hargreave shook himself like a man waking from a nightmare. "It's getting rather late," he said to Lilymary. "Perhaps—perhaps our guest would enjoy some coffee before he goes."

I declined the coffee and Lilymary walked me to the subway. We didn't talk much.

At the subway entrance she firmly took my hand and shook it. "It's been a pleasant evening," she said.

A wandering group of carolers came by; I gave my contribution to the guitarist. Suddenly angry, I said, "Doesn't that *mean* anything to you?"

"What?"

I gestured after the carolers. "That. Christmas. The whole sentimental, lovable, warmhearted business of Christmas. Lilymary, we've only known each other a short time, but—"

She interrupted: "Please, Mr. Martin. I—I know what you're going to say." She looked terribly appealing there in the Christmassy light of the red and green lights from the Tree that marked the subway entrance. Her pale, straight legs, hardly concealed by the shorts, picked up chromatic highlights; her eyes sparkled. She said. "You see, as Daddy says, we've been away from—civilization. Daddy is a missionary, and we've been with the Dyaks since I was a little girl. Gretch and Marlene and Corinne were born there. We—we do things differently on Borneo." She looked up at the Tree over us, and sighed. "It's very hard to get used to," she said. "Sometimes I wish we had stayed with the Dyaks."

Then she looked at me. She smiled. "But sometimes," she said, "I am very glad we're here." And she was gone.

Ambiguous? Call it merely ladylike. At any rate, that's what I called it; I took it to be the beginning of the kind of feeling I so desperately wanted her to have; and for the second night in a row I let Haroun's harem beauties remain silent on their tapes.

Calamity struck. My number-two man, Furness, turned up one morning with a dismal expression and a letter in a government-franked envelope. "Greeting!" it began. "You are summoned to serve with a jury of citizens for the term—"

"Jury duty!" I groaned. "At a time like this! Wait a minute, Johnny, I'll call up Mr. Heinemann. He might be able to fix it if—"

Furness was shaking his head. "Sorry, Mr. Martin. I already asked him and he tried; but no go. It's a big case—blindfold sampling of twelve brands of filter cigarettes—and Mr. Heinemann says it wouldn't look right to try to evade it."

So there was breaking another man in, to add to my troubles.

It meant overtime, and that meant that I didn't have as much time as I would like for Lilymary. Lunch together, a couple of times; odd moments between runs of the gift-wrapping machines; that was about it.

But she was never out of my thoughts. There was something about her that appealed to me. A square, yes. Unworldly, yes. Her family? A Victorian horror; but they were *her* family. I determined to get them on my side, and by and by I began to see how.

"Miss Hargreave," I said formally, coming out of

my office. We stepped to one side, in a corner under the delivery chutes. The rumble of goods overhead gave us privacy. I said, "Lilymary, you're taking this Sunday off, as usual? May I come to visit you?"

She hesitated only a second. "Why, of course," she said firmly. "We'd be delighted. For dinner?"

I shook my head: "I have a little surprise for you," I whispered. She looked alarmed. "Not for you, exactly. For the kids. Trust me, Lilymary. About four o'clock in the afternoon?"

I winked at her and went back to my office to make arrangements. It wasn't the easiest thing in the world—it was our busy season, as I say—but what's the use of being the boss if you can't pull rank once in a while? So I made it as strong as I could, and Special Services hemmed and hawed and finally agreed that they would work in a special Visit from Santa Claus at the Hargreave home that Sunday afternoon.

Once the kids were on my side, I plotted craftily, it would be easy enough to work the old man around, and what kid could resist a Visit from Santa Claus?

I rang the bell and walked into the queer South-Seas living room as though I belonged there. "Merry Christmas!" I said genially to the six-year-old who let me in. "I hope you kiddies are ready for a treat!"

She looked at me incredulously, and disappeared. I heard her say something shrill and protesting in the next room, and Lilymary's voice being firm and low-toned. Then Lilymary appeared. "Hello, Mr. Martin," she said.

"George."

"Hello, George." She sat down and patted the sofa

beside her. "Would you like some lemonade?" she asked.

"Thank you," I said. It was pretty hot for the end of September, and the place didn't appear to be air-conditioned. She called, and the twelve-year-old, Gretchen, turned up with a pitcher and some cookies. I said warningly:

"Mustn't get too full, little girl! There's a surprise coming."

Lilymary cleared her throat, as her sister set the tray down with a clatter and stamped out of the room. "I—I wish you'd tell me about this surprise, George," she said. "You know, we're a little, well, set in our ways, and I wonder—"

"Nothing to worry about, Lilymary," I reassured her. "What is it, a couple of minutes before four? They'll be here any minute."

"They?"

I looked around; the kids were out of sight. "Santa Claus and his helpers," I whispered.

She began piercingly: "Santa Cl—"

"Ssh!" I nodded toward the door. "I want it to be a surprise for the kids. Please don't spoil it for them, Lilymary."

Well, she opened her mouth; but she didn't get a chance to say anything. The bell rang; Santa Claus and his helpers were right on time.

"Lilymary!" shrieked the twelve-year-old, opening the door. "Look!"

You couldn't blame the kid for being excited. "Ho-ho-ho," boomed Santa, rolling inside. "Oh, hello, Mr. Martin. This the place?"

"Certainly, Santa," I said, beaming. "Bring it in, boys."

The twelve-year-old cried, "Corinne! Marlene! This you got to see!" There was an odd tone to her voice, but I didn't pay much attention. It wasn't my party any more. I retired, smiling, to a corner of the room while the Santa Claus helpers began coming in with their sacks of gear on their shoulders. It was "Ho-ho-ho, little girl!" and "Merry Christmas, everybody!" until you couldn't hear yourself think.

Lilymary was biting her lip, staring at me. The Santa tapped her on the shoulder. "Where's the kitchen, lady?" he asked. "That door? Okay, Wynken—go on in and get set up. Nod, you go down and hurry up the sound truck, then you can handle the door. The rest of you helpers—" he surveyed the room briefly— "start lining up your Christmas Goodies there, and there. Now hop to it, boys! We got four more Visits to make this afternoon yet."

You never saw a crew of Christmas Gnomes move as fast as them. Snap, and the Tree was up, complete with its tinsel stars and gray colored Order Forms and Credit Application Blanks. Snip, and two of the helpers were stringing the red and green lights that led from the Hargreave living room to the sound truck outside. Snip-snap, and you could hear the sound truck pealing the joyous strains of *All I Want for Christmas Is Two of Everything* in the street, and twos and threes of the neighborhood children were beginning to appear at the door, blinking and ready for the fun. The kitchen helpers were lading out mugs of cocoa and colored-sugar Christmas cookies and collecting the dimes and quarters from the kids; the demonstrator helpers were showing the kids the toys and trinkets from their sacks; and Santa himself was seated on his glittering throne. "Ho-ho-ho, my boy," he was saying. "And where does your daddy work this merry Christmas season?"

I was proud of them. There wasn't a helper there who couldn't have walked into Saul & Cappell or any other store in town, and walked out a Santa with a crew of his own. But that's the way we do things at the Emporium, skilled hands and high paychecks, and you only have to look at our sales records to see that it pays off.

Well, I wanted to stay and watch the fun, but Sunday's a bad day to take the afternoon off; I slipped out and headed back to the store. I put in a hard four hours, but I made it a point to be down at the Special Services division when the crews came straggling in for their checkout. The crew I was interested in was the last to report, naturally—isn't that always the way? Santa was obviously tired; I let him shuck his uniform and turn his sales slips in to the cashier before I tackled him. "How did it go?" I asked anxiously. "Did Miss Hargreave—I mean the grown-up Miss Hargreave— did she say anything?"

He looked at me accusingly. "You," he whined. "Mr. Martin, you shouldn't have run out on us like that. How we supposed to keep up a schedule when you throw us that kind of a curve, Mr. Martin?"

It was no way for a Santa to be talking to a department head, but I overlooked it. The man was obviously upset. "What are you talking about?" I demanded.

"Those Hargreaves! Honestly, Mr. Martin, you'd think they didn't want us there, the way they acted! The kids were bad enough. But when the old man came home—wow! I tell you, Mr. Martin, I been eleven Christmases in the Department, and I never saw a family with less Christmas spirit than those Hargreaves!"

The cashier was yelling for the cash receipts so he could lock up his ledgers for the night, so I let the Santa go. But I had plenty to think about as I went back to my own department, wondering about what he had said.

I didn't have to wonder long. Just before closing, one of the office girls waved me in from where I was checking out a new Counselor, and I answered the phone call. It was Lilymary's father. Mad? He was blazing. I could hardly make sense out of most of what he said. It was words like "perverting the Christian festival" and "selling out the Saviour" and a lot of stuff I just couldn't follow at all. But the part he finished up with, that I could understand. "I want you to know, Mr. Martin," he said in clear, crisp, emphatic tones, "that you are no longer a welcome caller at our home. It pains me to have to say this, sir. As for Lilymary, you may consider this her resignation, to be effective at once!"

"But," I said, "but—"

But I was talking to a dead line; he had hung up. And that was the end of that.

Personnel called up after a couple of days and wanted to know what to do with Lilymary's severance pay. I told them to mail her the check; then I had a second thought and asked them to send it up to me. I mailed it to her myself, with a little note apologizing for what I'd done wrong—whatever it was. But she didn't even answer.

October began, and the pace stepped up. Every

night I crawled home, bone-weary, turned on my dreamster and slept like a log. I gave the machine a real workout; I even had the buyer in the Sleep Shoppe get me rare, out-of-print tapes on special order—Last Days of Petronius Arbiter, and Casanova's Diary, and The Polly Adler Story, and so on—until the buyer began to leer when she saw me coming. But it didn't do any good. While I slept I was surrounded with the loveliest of them all; but when I woke the face of Lilymary Hargreave was in my mind's eye.

October. The store was buzzing. National cost of living was up .00013, but our rate of sale was up .00021 over the previous year. The store bosses were beaming, and bonuses were in the air for everybody. November. The tide was at its full, and little wavelets began to ebb backward. Housewares was picked clean, and the manufacturers only laughed as we implored them for deliveries; but Home Appliances was as dead as the January lull. Our overall rate of sale slowed down microscopically, but it didn't slow down the press of work. It made things tougher, in fact, because we were pushing twice as hard on the items we could supply, coaxing the customers off the ones that were running short.

Bad management? No. Looking at my shipment figures, we'd actually emptied the store four times in seven weeks—better than fifty per cent turnover a week. Our July purchase estimates had been off only slightly—two persons fewer out of each hundred bought air-conditioners than we had expected, one and a half persons more out of each hundred bought kitchenware. Saul & Cappell had been out of kitchenware except for spot deliveries, sold the day they arrived, ever since late September!

Heinemann called me into his office. "George," he said, "I just checked your backlog. The unfilled order list runs a little over eleven thousand. I want to tell you that I'm surprised at the way you and your department have—"

"Now, Mr. Heinemann!" I burst out. "That isn't fair! We've been putting in overtime every night, every blasted one of us! Eleven thousand's pretty good, if you ask me!"

He looked surprised. "My point exactly, George," he said. "I was about to compliment you."

I felt *so* high. I swallowed. "Uh, thanks," I said. "I mean, I'm sorry I—"

"Forget it. George." Heinemann was looking at me thoughtfully. "You've got something on your mind, don't you?"

"Well—"

"Is it that girl?"

"Girl?" I stared at him. "Who said anything about a girl?"

"Come off it," he said genially. "You think it isn't all over the store?" He glanced at his watch. "George," he said, "I never interfere in employees' private lives. You know that. But if it's that girl that's bothering you, why don't you marry her for a while? It might be just the thing you need. Come on now. George, confess. When were you married last? Three years? Five years ago?"

I looked away. "I never was," I admitted.

That jolted him. "Never?" He studied me thoughtfully for a second. "You aren't—?"

"No, no, no!" I said hastily. "Nothing like that. It's

just that, well, it's always seemed like a pretty big step to take."

He relaxed again. "Ah, you kids," he said genially. "Always afraid of getting hurt, eh? Well, I'll mind my own business, if that's the way you want it. But if I were you, George, I'd go get her."

That was that. I went back to work; but I kept right on thinking about what Heinemann had said.

After all . . . why not?

I called, "Lilymary!"

She faltered and half-turned. I had counted on that. You could tell she wasn't brought up in this country; from the age of six on, our girls learn Lesson One: When you're walking alone at night, *don't stop*.

She didn't stop long. She peered into the doorway and saw me, and her expression changed as though I had hit her with a club. "George," she said, and hesitated, and walked on. Her hair was a shimmering rainbow in the Christmas lights.

We were only a few doors from her house. I glanced, half-apprehensive, at the door, but no Father Hargreave was there to scowl. I followed her and said, "Please, Lilymary. Can't we just talk for a moment?"

She faced me. "Why?"

"To—" I swallowed. "To let me apologize."

She said gently, "No apology is necessary, George. We're different breeds of cats. No need to apologize for that."

"*Please*."

"Well," she said. And then, "Why not?"

We found a bench in the little park across from the subway entrance. It was late; enormous half-tracks from the Sanitation Department were emptying trash cans, sprinkler trucks came by and we had to raise our feet off the ground. She said once, "I really ought to get back. I was only going to the store." But she stayed.

Well, I apologized, and she listened like a lady. And like a lady she said, again, "There's nothing to apologize for." And that was that, and I still hadn't said what I had come for. I didn't know how.

I brooded over the problem. With the rumble of the trash trucks and the roar of their burners, conversation was difficult enough anyhow. But even under those handicaps, I caught a phrase from Lilymary. "—back to the jungle," she was saying. "It's home for us, George. Father can't wait to get back, and neither can the girls."

I interrupted her. "Get back?"

She glanced at me. "That's what I said." She nodded at the Sanitation workers, baling up the enormous drifts of Christmas cards, thrusting them into the site burners. "As soon as the mails open up," she said, "and Father gets his visa. It was mailed a week ago, they say. They tell me that in the Christmas rush it might take two or three weeks more to get to us, though."

Something was clogging up my throat. All I could say was, "Why?"

Lilymary sighed. "It's where we live, George," she explained. "This isn't right for us. We're mission brats and we belong out in the field, spreading the Good News.... Though Father says you people need it more than the Dyaks." She looked quickly into my eyes. "I mean—"

I waved it aside. I took a deep breath. "Lilymary," I said, all in a rush, "will you marry me?"

Silence, while Lilymary looked at me.

"Oh, George," she said, after a moment. And that was all; but I was able to translate it; the answer was no.

Still, proposing marriage is something like buying a lottery ticket; you may not win the grand award, but there are consolation prizes. Mine was a date.

Lilymary stood up to her father, and I was allowed in the house. I wouldn't say I was welcomed, but Dr. Hargreave was polite—distant, but polite. He offered me coffee, he spoke of the dream superstitions of the Dyaks and old days in the Long House, and when Lilymary was ready to go he shook my hand at the door.

We had dinner. . . . I asked her—but as a piece of conversation, not a begging plea from the heart—I asked her why they had to go back. The Dyaks, she said; they were Father's people; they needed him. After Mother's death, Father had wanted to come back to America . . . but it was wrong for them. He was going back. The girls, naturally, were going with him.

We danced. . . . I kissed her, in the shadows, when it was growing late. She hesitated, but she kissed me back.

I resolved to destroy my dreamster; its ersatz ecstasies were pale.

"There," she said, as she drew back, and her voice was gentle, with a note of laughter. "I just wanted to show you. It isn't all hymn-singing back on Borneo, you know."

I reached out for her again, but she drew back, and the laughter was gone. She glanced at her watch.

"Time for me to go, George," she said. "We start packing tomorrow."

"But—"

"It's time to go, George," she said. And she kissed me at her door; but she didn't invite me in.

I stripped the tapes off my dreamster and threw them away. But hours later, after the fiftieth attempt to get to sleep, and the twentieth solitary cigarette, I got up and turned on the light and looked for them again.

They were pale; but they were all I had.

Party Week! The store was nearly bare. A messenger from the Credit Department came staggering in with a load of files just as the closing gong sounded.

He dropped them on my desk. "Thank God!" he said fervently. "Guess you won't be bothering with these tonight, eh, Mr. Martin?"

But I searched through them all the same. He looked at me wonderingly, but the clerks were breaking out the bottles and the runners from the lunchroom were bringing up sandwiches, and he drifted away.

I found the credit check I had requested. "*Co-Maker Required!*" was stamped at the top, and triply underlined in red, but that wasn't what I was looking for. I hunted through the text until I found what I wanted to know: "Subject is expected to leave this country within forty-eight hours. Subject's employer is organized and incorporated under laws of State of New York as a religious mission group. No earnings record on file. *Caution:* Subject would appear a bad credit risk, due to—"

I read no farther. Forty-eight hours!

There was a scrawl at the bottom of the page, in the Credit Manager's own handwriting: "George, what the devil are you up to? This is the fourth check we made on these people!"

It was true enough; but it would be the last. In forty-eight hours they would be gone.

I was dull at the Christmas Party. But it had been a splendid Christmas for the store, and in an hour everyone was too drunk to notice.

I decided to skip Party Week. I stayed at home the next morning, staring out the window. It had begun to snow, and the cleaners were dragging away old Christmas trees. It's always a letdown when Christmas is over; but my mood had nothing to do with the season, only with Lilymary and the numbers of miles from here to Borneo.

I circled the date in red on my calendar: December 25th. By the 26th they would be gone....

But I couldn't, repeat couldn't, let her go so easily. It wasn't that I wanted to try again, and be rebuffed again; it was not a matter of choice. I had to see her. Nothing else, suddenly, had any meaning. So I made the long subway trek out there, knowing it was a fool's errand. But what kind of an errand could have been more appropriate for me?

They weren't home, but I wasn't going to let that stop me. I banged on the door of the next apartment, and got a surly, suspicious, what-do-you-want-with-*them*? inspection from the woman who lived there. But she thought they might possibly be down at the Community Center on the next block.

And they were.

The Community Center was a big yellow-brick rec-

reation hall; it had swimming pools and pingpong
tables and all kinds of odds and ends to keep the kids
off the streets. It was that kind of a neighborhood. It
also had a meeting hall in the basement, and there
were the Hargreaves, all of them, along with a couple
of dozen other people. None of them were young,
except the Hargreave girls. The hall had a dusty,
storeroom quality to it, as though it wasn't used
much—and in fact, I saw, it still had a small Christmas
tree standing in it. Whatever else they had, they did
not have a very efficient cleanup squad.

I came to the door to the hall and stood there,
looking around. Someone was playing a piano, and
they were having a singing party. The music sounded
familiar, but I couldn't recognize the words—

> *Adeste fideles,*
> *Laeti triumphantes.*
> *Venite, venite in Bethlehem.*

The girls were sitting together, in the front row;
their father wasn't with them, but I saw why. He was
standing at a little lectern in the front of the hall.

> *Natum videte, regem angelorum.*
> *Venite adoremus, venite adoremus—*

I recognized the tune then; it was a slow, draggy-
beat steal from that old-time favorite, *Christmas-Tree
Mambo*. It didn't sound too bad, though, as they finished with a big major chord from the piano and all
fifteen or twenty voices going. Then Hargreave
started to talk.

I didn't listen. I was too busy watching the back of

Lilymary's head. I've always had pretty low psi, though, and she didn't turn around.

Something was bothering me. There was a sort of glow from up front. I took my eyes off Lilymary's blond head, and there was Dr. Hargreave, radiant; I blinked and looked again, and it was not so radiant. A trick of the light, coming through the basement windows onto his own blond hair, I suppose, but it gave me a curious feeling for a moment. I must have moved, because he caught sight of me. He stumbled over a word, but then he went on. But that was enough. After a moment Lilymary's head turned, and her eyes met mine.

She knew I was there. I backed away from the door and sat down on the steps coming down from the entrance.

Sooner or later she would be out.

It wasn't long at all. She came toward me with a question in her eye. She was all by herself; inside the hall, her father was still talking.

I stood up straight and said it all. "Lilymary," I said, "I can't help it, I want to marry you. I've done everything wrong, but I didn't mean to. I—I don't even want it conditional, Lilymary, I want it for life. Here or Borneo, I don't care which. I only care about one thing, and that's you." It was funny—I was trying to tell her I loved her, and I was standing stiff and awkward, talking in about the same tone of voice I'd use to tell a stock boy he was fired.

But she understood. I probably didn't have to say a word, she would have understood anyhow. She started to speak, and changed her mind, and started again, and finally got out, "What would you do in

Borneo?" And then, so soft that I hardly knew I was hearing it, she added, "Dear."

Dear! It was like the first time Heinemann came in and called me "Department Head!" I felt nine feet tall.

I didn't answer her. I reached out and I kissed her, and it wasn't any wonder that I didn't know we weren't alone until I heard her father cough, not more than a yard away.

I jumped, but Lilymary turned and looked at him, perfectly calm. "You ought to be conducting the service, Father!" she scolded him.

He nodded his big fair head. "Doctor Mausner can pronounce the Benediction without me," he said. "I should be there but—well, He has plenty of things to forgive all of us already; one more isn't going to bother Him. Now, what's this?"

"George has asked me to marry him."

"And?"

She looked at me. "I—" she began, and stopped. I said, "I love her."

He looked at me too, and then he sighed. "George," he said after a moment, "I don't know what's right and what's wrong, for the first time in my life. Maybe I've been selfish when I asked Lilymary to go back with me and the girls. I didn't mean it that way, but I don't deny I wanted it. I don't know. But—" He smiled, and it was a big, warm smile. "But there's something I do know. I know Lilymary; and I can trust her to make up her own mind." He patted her lightly.

"I'll see you after the service," he said to me, and left us. Back in the hall, through the door he opened, I could hear all the voices going at once.

"Let's go inside and pray, George," said Lilymary, and her whole heart and soul was on her face as she looked at me, with love and anxiousness.

I only hesitated a moment. Pray? But it meant Lilymary, and that meant—well, everything.

So I went in. And we were all kneeling, and Lilymary coached me through the words; and I prayed. And, do you know?—I've never regretted it.

The War Beneath the Tree

Gene Wolfe

"It's Christmas Eve, Commander Robin," the Space-man said. "You'd better go to bed, or Santa won't come."

Robin's mother said, "That's right, Robin. Time to say good night."

The little boy in blue pajamas nodded, but made no move to rise.

"Kiss me," said Bear. Bear walked his funny, waddly walk around the tree and threw his arms about Robin. "We have to go to bed. I'll come too." It was what he said every night.

Robin's mother shook her head in amused despair. "Listen to them," she said. "Look at him, Bertha. He's like a little prince surrounded by his court. How is he going to feel when he's grown and can't have tran-sistorized sycophants to spoil him all the time?"

Bertha the robot maid nodded her own almost human head as she put the poker back in its stand. "That's right, Ms. Jackson. That's right for sure."

The Dancing Doll took Robin by the hand, making an *arabesque penché* of it. Now Robin rose. His guardsmen formed up and presented arms.

"On the other hand," Robin's mother said, "they're children only such a short time."

Bertha nodded again. "They're only young once, Ms. Jackson. That's for sure. All right if I tell these little cute toys to help me straighten up after he's asleep?"

The Captain of the Guardsmen saluted with his silver saber, the Largest Guardsman beat the tattoo on his drum, and the rest of the guardsmen formed a double file.

"He sleeps with Bear," Robin's mother said.

"I can spare Bear. There's plenty of others."

The Spaceman touched the buckle of his antigravity belt and soared to a height of four feet like a graceful, broad-shouldered balloon. With the Dancing Doll on his left and Bear on his right, Robin toddled off behind the guardsmen. Robin's mother ground out her last cigarette of the evening, winked at Bertha, and said, "I suppose I'd better turn in too. You needn't help me undress, just pick up my things in the morning."

"Yes'um. Too bad Mr. Jackson ain't here, it bein' Christmas Eve and you expectin' an' all."

"He'll be back from Brazil in a week—I've told you already. And Bertha, your speech habits are getting worse and worse. Are you sure you wouldn't rather be a French maid for a while?"

"Maize none, Ms. Jackson. I have too much trouble

talkin' to the men that comes to the door when I'm French."

"When Mr. Jackson gets his next promotion, we're going to have a chauffeur," Robin's mother said. "He's going to be Italian, and he's going to *stay* Italian."

Bertha watched her waddle out of the room. "All right, you lazy toys! You empty them ashtrays into the fire an' get everythin' put away. I'm goin' to turn myself off, but the next time I come on, this room better be straight or there's goin' to be some broken toys around here."

She watched long enough to see the Gingham Dog dump the largest ashtray on the crackling logs, the Spaceman float up to straighten the magazines on the coffee table, and the Dancing Doll begin to sweep the hearth. "Put yourselfs in your box," she told the guardsmen, and turned off.

In the smallest bedroom, Bear lay in Robin's arm. "Be quiet," said Robin.

"I *am* quiet," said Bear.

"Every time I am almost gone to sleep, you squiggle."

"I don't," said Bear.

"You do."

"Sometimes you have trouble going to sleep too, Robin," said Bear.

"I'm having trouble *tonight*," Robin countered meaningfully.

Bear slipped from under his arm. "I want to see if it's snowing again." He climbed from the bed to an open drawer, and from the open drawer to the top of the dresser. It was snowing.

Robin said, "Bear, you have a circuit loose." It was

what his mother sometimes said to Bertha.

Bear did not reply.

"Oh, Bear," Robin said sleepily, a moment later. "I know why you're antsy. It's your birthday tomorrow, and you think I didn't get you anything."

"Did you?" Bear asked.

"I will," Robin said. "Mother will take me to the store." In half a minute his breathing became the regular, heavy sighing of a sleeping child.

Bear sat on the edge of the dresser and looked at him. Then he said under his breath, "I can sing Christmas carols." It had been the first thing he had ever said to Robin, one year ago. He spread his arms. *All is calm. All is bright.* It made him think of the lights on the tree and the bright fire in the living room. The Spaceman was there, but because he was the only toy who could fly, none of the others liked the Spaceman much. The Dancing Doll was there too. The Dancing Doll was clever, but, well . . . He could not think of the word.

He jumped down into the drawer on top of a pile of Robin's undershirts, then out of the drawer, softly to the dark, carpeted floor.

"Limited," he said to himself. "The Dancing Doll is limited." He thought again of the fire, then of the old toys, the Blocks Robin had had before he and the Dancing Doll and the rest had come—the Wooden Man who rode a yellow bicycle, the Singing Top.

In the living room, the Dancing Doll was positioning the guardsmen, while the Spaceman stood on the mantel and supervised. "We can get three or four behind the bookcase," he called.

"Where they won't be able to see a thing," Bear growled.

The Dancing Doll pirouetted and dropped a sparkling curtsy. "We were afraid you wouldn't come," she said.

"Put one behind each leg of the coffee table," Bear told her. "I had to wait until he was asleep. Now listen to me, all of you. When I call, *'Charge!'* we must all run at them together. That's very important. If we can, we'll have a practice beforehand."

The Largest Guardsman said, "I'll beat my drum."

"You'll beat the enemy, or you'll go into the fire with the rest of us," Bear said.

Robin was sliding on the ice. His feet went out from under him and right up into the air so he fell down with a tremendous BUMP that shook him all over. He lifted his head, and he was not on the frozen pond in the park at all. He was in his own bed, with the moon shining in at the window, and it was Christmas Eve...no, Christmas Night now...and Santa was coming, maybe had already come. Robin listened for reindeer on the roof and did not hear reindeer steps. Then he listened for Santa eating the cookies his mother had left on the stone shelf by the fireplace. There was no munching or crunching. Then he threw back the covers and slipped down over the edge of his bed until his feet touched the floor. The good smells of tree and fire had come into his room. He followed them out of it ever so quietly, into the hall.

Santa was in the living room, bent over beside the tree! Robin's eyes opened until they were as big and as round as his pajama buttons. Then Santa straightened up, and he was not Santa at all, but Robin's mother in a new red bathrobe. Robin's mother was nearly as fat as Santa, and Robin had to put his fingers in his mouth to keep from laughing at the way she puffed, and pushed at her knees with her hands until she stood straight.

But Santa had come! There were toys—new toys!—everywhere under the tree.

Robin's mother went to the cookies on the stone shelf and ate half of one. Then she drank half the glass of milk. Then she turned to go back into her bedroom, and Robin retreated into the darkness of his own room until she was past. When he peeked cautiously around the door frame again, the toys—the new toys—were beginning to move.

They shifted and shook themselves and looked about. Perhaps it was because it was Christmas Eve. Perhaps it was only because the light of the fire had activated their circuits. But a Clown brushed himself off and stretched, and a Raggedy Girl smoothed her raggedy apron (with the heart embroidered on it), and a Monkey gave a big jump and chinned himself on the next-to-lowest limb of the Christmas tree. Robin saw them. And Bear, behind the hassock of Robin's father's chair, saw them too. Cowboys and Native Americans were lifting the lid of a box, and a Knight opened a cardboard door (made to look like wood) in the side of another box (made to look like stone), letting a Dragon peer over his shoulder.

"Charge!" Bear called. *"Charge!"* He came around the side of the hassock on all fours like a real bear, running stiffly but very fast, and he hit the Clown at his wide waistline and knocked him down, then picked him up and threw him halfway to the fire.

The Spaceman had swooped down on the Monkey;

they wrestled, teetering, on top of a polystyrene tricycle.

The Dancing Doll had charged fastest of all, faster even than Bear himself, in a breathtaking series of *jetés*, but the Raggedy Girl had lifted her feet from the floor, and now she was running with her toward the fire. As Bear struck the Clown a second time, he saw two Native Americans carrying a guardsman— the Captain of the Guardsmen—toward the fire too. The Captain's saber had gone through one of the Native Americans and it must have disabled some circuit because the Native American walked badly; but in a moment more the Captain was burning, his red uniform burning, his hands thrown up like flames themselves, his black eyes glazing and cracking, bright metal running from him like sweat to harden among the ashes under the logs.

The Clown tried to wrestle with Bear, but Bear threw him down. The Dragon's teeth were sunk in Bear's left heel, but he kicked himself free. The Calico Cat was burning, burning. The Gingham Dog tried to pull her out, but the Monkey pushed him in. For a moment, Bear thought of the cellar stairs and the deep, dark cellar, where there were boxes and bundles and a hundred forgotten corners. If he ran and hid, the new toys might never find him, might never even try to find him. Years from now Robin would discover him, covered with dust.

The Dancing Doll's scream was high and sweet, and Bear turned to face the Knight's upraised sword.

When Robin's mother got up on Christmas Morning, Robin was awake already, sitting under the tree with the Cowboys, watching the Native Americans do their rain dance. The Monkey was perched on his shoulder, the Raggedy Girl (programmed, the store had assured Robin's mother, to begin Robin's sex education) in his lap, and the Knight and the Dragon were at his feet. "Do you like the toys Santa brought you, Robin?" Robin's mother asked.

"One of the Native Amer'cans doesn't work."

"Never mind, dear, we'll take him back. Robin, I've got something important to tell you."

Bertha the robot maid came in with Corn Flakes and milk and vitamins, and café au lait for Robin's mother. "Where is those old toys?" she asked. "They done a picky-poor job of cleanin' up this room."

"Robin, your toys are just toys, of course—"

Robin nodded absently. A Red Calf was coming out of the chute, with a Cowboy on a Roping Horse after him.

"Where *is* those old toys, Ms. Jackson?" Bertha asked again.

"They're programmed to self-destruct, I understand," Robin's mother said. "But, Robin, you know how the new toys all came, the Knight and Dragon and all your Cowboys, almost by magic? Well, the same thing can happen with people."

Robin looked at her with frightened eyes.

"The same wonderful thing is going to happen here, in our home."

The Santa Claus Planet

Frank M. Robinson

"I think the town is over this way, sir," Hawsworthy said, his words coming out in little puffs of steam.

Leftenant Harkins waited until there was a brief calm in the flurries of snow whirling about him, then shielded his eyes and and stared in the direction that Hawsworthy had pointed. There was a small cluster of lights in the distance—a good two or three snowy miles away, he judged sourly—but it couldn't be anything but the twinkling lights of some primitive village.

He sighed and pulled the collar of his heavy tunic tighter around his neck, then turned for a last look at the *Churchill*, the sleek and shiny line-cruiser bulking huge in the valley a few hundred yards to the rear. Her ports were radiating a cozy, yellow warmth and he could catch glimpses of her officers and enlisted men standing around the brightly bedecked tree

119

in the main lounge. He even fancied that he could hear the strains of *Cantique Noel* and smell the hot, spicy odor of the wassail drifting up on the cold, sharp air.

Christmas Eve . . .

He bit his thin lips in disappointment. Outside in the cold on a fool's errand while inside the *Churchill* the Christmas celebration was just getting started. He had done the best he could in making arrangements with Ensign Jarvis to save him some of the wassail, but knowing Jarvis' own enthusiasm for the monthly liquor ration, they were shaky arrangements at best.

A sudden gust of snow hid the ship and he and Hawsworthy wheeled and started trudging towards the faint glow on the horizon.

It was traditional in the service, Harkins thought, to set the ship down on some hospitable planet for Christmas. Christmas wasn't Christmas without the solid feeling of the good earth under you and the smell of pine and the soft mistiness of snow drifting gently down from the sky.

Naturally, there had been a lot of enthusiasm aboard ship. The commissary had been busy all week filling the ship with the appetizing odors of synthetic roast goose and plum pudding and the pleasant spiciness of fruit cakes. And the carpentry shop had spent many a hard afternoon building the tree out of fine dowels and daubing it with green paint, just in case they were unable to obtain the genuine article.

Then—only an hour ago, Harkins thought bitterly—the captain had asked to see him and his own personal enthusiasm had collapsed like a pricked balloon.

The captain had discovered that the planet supported a human culture, so it was naturally incumbent on the *Churchill* to send forth a deputation to invite members of the Terran speaking community—if any—aboard to celebrate Christmas with the crew, present the ship's credentials to the powers that might be, and try and arrange for possible planet leave.

And as he had once dabbled in anthropology, the deputation was to be made in the person of Leftenant Junior Grade Harkins. Which meant that he would miss most of the celebration. On top of that, he had drawn Hawsworthy for an assistant. (There was nothing wrong with Hawsworthy, of course, except that he had an amazing talent for making you feel ill at ease and unsure of yourself. He was a twenty-year man and you always suspected that his feelings towards the junior grades were composed more of toleration than respect.)

"It can't be much further, sir. I think I can make out some of the buildings." The lights of the town were considerably nearer now and the rough shapes of small houses had begun to separate themselves from the snow-filled blackness.

A fool's errand, Harkins thought for the twentieth time. The records showed that the people were nothing but primitives, but that hadn't prevented the captain from doing "the decent thing" and sending out a representative anyways. Tradition. The people were probably fish-eaters, and any authority to which he might present the ship's credentials undoubtedly resided in the painted and scarred body of the village witch doctor, probably hiding under his cooking pot right then.

Then they were on the summit of the last hill before the town, gazing down at the village below; a village where the streets were neatly laid out, the houses were a large cut above the usual thatched or skin affair, and primitive arc-lamps were strung across the snowy streets.

Harkins felt uneasy. It wasn't at all as primitive as it should be.

They walked into the seemingly deserted town and had proceeded a few blocks when Hawsworthy suddenly stopped and pulled out his pistol. "Something's coming, Leftenant."

Harkins' heart rose into his mouth. There was a measured tread of feet down a side street, and a moment later a procession marched into view. Four natives dressed in rich furs were in the van and behind them came an opulently decorated sleigh, pulled by a large, splay-footed animal. The procession halted and four natives in front bowed low.

For the first time, Harkins noticed that they were carrying what were obviously meant to be gifts. Huge, circular sheets of beaten copper with crude designs hammered in them, and hampers containing what looked like carcasses of not-too-recently slaughtered alley cats. The natives straightened up and proffered the gifts, then backed away, obviously expectant.

Harkins accepted the gifts awkwardly, after which there was a long and increasingly heavy silence. Finally a voice from within the sleigh spoke.

"Don't just stand there—destroy the gifts, then hand them your pistols."

Harkins gasped. The voice spoke his own tongue excellently.

Hawsworthy chewed his lower lip and looked belligerent. "If we do, sir, we'll be unarmed and at their mercy. I wouldn't advise it."

"Please show yourself," Harkins said to the curtained sleigh.

The curtains parted and a man stepped out. He was plump and betrayed the usual signs of easy living but his eyes were alive and his face showed a familiar ruddiness. The Terran type, Harkins thought, amazed; he showed it distinctly.

"Do as I tell you and nothing will happen to you," the man urged.

"We would like to see your ruler," Harkins said stiffly, thinking of an alternative.

The fat man put his hands on his hips and cocked his head at them. "You're looking at him. The name's Harry Reynolds and I run this planet—at least, this section of it."

Harkins digested this in silence, then awoke to his responsibilities as a representative of the *Churchill* and introduced himself and Hawsworthy.

"You're sure no harm will come of this?"

"My word," Reynolds said expansively.

Harkins pondered for a moment, then flamed the copper shields and the hampers and handed over his pistol. Hawsworthy did the same. The natives smiled, stripped the cartridges from the pistols, broke the plastic barrels, and finally bowed low and withdrew.

It was then that it occurred to Harkins that things were looking up. The natives were friendly, a Terrestrial was running things, and chances for planet leave looked highly probable.

Then another thought hit him. He turned to Reynolds and saluted. "Sir, the officers and men of the *Churchill* would be highly complimented if you consented to celebrate Christmas with them on board ship."

Reynolds accepted with alacrity and Harkins gestured to the sleigh. "I'd suggest using your sleigh, sir; we'd save time."

Later, seated on the warm cushions of the sleigh and skimming over the countryside, Harkins reflected proudly that his commandeering of the sleigh was a master stroke. Not only was Hawsworthy duly impressed with his quick thinking, but it looked highly possible that they'd get back to the ship before Jarvis had had a chance to consume all the wassail.

It was going to be a pleasant evening at that, he thought, and not the least of its pleasantness was going to be when he pinned Reynolds down and found out just how he happened to be running things.

He looked at Reynolds' ruddy face out of the corner of his eye. There was probably quite a story to it.

Back in the *Churchill*, the junior grades soon had Reynolds surrounded.

"What do you call this planet, Mr. Reynolds?" Jarvis asked, glass in hand. "Something quite different than the numbers and letters the star maps give it, I imagine."

Reynolds ran a finger down the side of his nose and looked thoughtful. "The first few weeks I was here, I thought that I would call it the 'Santa Claus Planet.'"

Jarvis looked puzzled. "The Santa Claus Planet?"

"Yes. You see, the natives had made quite a ceremony out of giving gifts—but that's all part of the story."

Harkins seized the opening. "Tell us about it. Back in the town, you said you ran this section of the planet. I couldn't help but wonder just how you did it."

Reynolds filled his glass again. "You can chalk it up to imagination—and quite a dose of plain, dumb luck.

It started about thirty years ago, when I was returning to Canopus from a business trip. My tubes blew and I had to make a forced landing on this planet. Naturally, I was stranded until I could make repairs..."

Reynolds groaned and slowly opened his eyes. The cabin seemed to be spinning tightly around him and he fought for control of his stomach, then gave up the struggle and turned on his side and let everything come up. After that, the feeling of nausea gradually passed and the cabin settled down, but it settled at a thirty-degree slant. He vaguely recalled the crash and rolled his eyes slightly to take in all of the cabin. What loose equipment and furnishings there were had been swept down the inclined deck to come to a rest in a broken, jumbled mass against the far bulkhead; he couldn't tell what other damage there might be but thin curls of blue smoke were drifting up from the engine room—the slightly acrid smoke of burning insulation.

But the ship was still whole, he thought grimly, and he was still alive, which was a wonder considering that he had been juggled around the inside of the rocket like a pair of dice in a shaker. He moved one arm experimentally and then the other. They were stiff and sore and blood had dried on a few nasty looking cuts, but no bones were broken.

The feeling of nausea hit him again and he retched, then gathered his courage and staggered to his rubbery legs. The port on the side of the cabin nearest the ground was shattered and fresh, cool air was blowing through the opening. It smelled good and helped clear more of the cobwebs from his head. Inspection of the hatch a moment later showed that it was hopelessly stuck so he found a broken hand-rail and laboriously battered out the fragments of quartz still in the port, then painfully crawled through and dropped to the grassy ground below.

He lay where he had fallen collecting his strength, then stumbled over to a stream not far from the ship. Half his shirt served as a washrag to help scrub off the grease and grime and clean his wounds; out of the other half he made crude bandages. He was gasping from weariness when he finished and slumped down on the bank to take stock of his situation.

The task of repairing the ship wasn't an impossible one—maybe two weeks, maybe less. In the meantime, he was stranded on the planet.

He found a self-lighter cigarette in his pants and drew in on it, watching the tip turn to a cherry red coal.

Stranded.

But he couldn't have been stranded in a better place, he reasoned. He had crashed in a low, broad valley with the stream running through the center of it. A carpet of grass dotted with the pink of some alien flower covered most of the ground, while surrounding the valley were low hills and forests of huge, fernlike trees. The weather seemed warm and temperate and the sky was a rich, tropical blue, with fleecy shreds of clouds drifting slowly by.

He brushed a lock of thinning black hair away from the bandage wrapped around his head and frowned. According to his star map, the natives were human—probably the degenerate remnants of those who had colonized the planet hundreds of years ago—but friendly.

At least they better be, he thought; there weren't

any weapons on board ship to speak of.

The warm sun made him drowsy and he let his thoughts wander where they would. Two weeks here and then off to Canopus where a somewhat shrewish wife and his small, sickly daughter would undoubtedly demand a long and detailed explanation of what had kept him. They would probably refuse to believe a truthful story about blown tubes so he would have to devote a part of his next two weeks to fabricating a wildly implausible and slightly incriminating story that they *would* believe.

But until then, he had two weeks of hard work and solitude ahead of him. In a way, a very pleasant vacation.

He plucked a blade of green grass from the side of the bank and chewed on it for a while. The work could commence tomorrow; he'd have to rest and recuperate today.

He turned on his side and dozed the rest of the day.

The sun had barely risen the next morning when Reynolds was up and inspecting the damage done to the ship. The bottom jets were fused and crumpled, the generators would have to be rewound, and stanchions and handrails and brackets on the inside would have to be welded back in place.

He got a shovel from inside the ship and walked around to the tube assembly, the dew on the grass dampening his canvas work shoes. It might be wise, he thought, to dig a hole under the rear jets, leaving the rocket balanced on a ridge of earth, so he could get at them. That would be the biggest job and the most difficult, and next to the generators, the most important.

He shifted awkwardly in his overalls, then pushed the shovel into the ground, heaved, and threw the dirt over his shoulder. It was rich, fertile looking loam which looked as if it had never been farmed. The people were probably strictly a hunting society...

The sun was hot and he found he had to take frequent rests from the digging. He had never been the muscular type in the first place and with his arms as sore as they were, it was tough going. But by noon, he had worked himself into a pit about waist-level and by late afternoon, he was shoulder-deep. He had long since taken off his heavy, twill work shirt and the sweat had soaked into the undershirt and burned into some of the cuts that hadn't healed yet.

There were two feet to go before the tubes would be completely unearthed, but he had to rest. He ached in a million places and blisters had formed, broken, and reformed on his swollen hands. He put the shovel to one side and sank quietly down on the cool dirt.

Five minutes later there was the quiet pad of feet above him and a soft voice said: "We bring presents for the man from the rocket."

He looked up, startled, his hand clutching the shovel for a possible weapon.

There were three of them at the top of the pit. Two of them were alert-eyed, bronzed men, dressed in richly decorated animal hides. They were inspecting him curiously, but not with the curiosity of natives who had never seen strangers before. Reynolds guessed, and rightly, that there had been visitors to the planet in the past.

The third member of the party—the one who had

spoken to him and apparently the only one who understood his language—was a rather pretty girl with the soft, rounded features that so many native girls seem to have. He looked at her with more than casual interest, noting that her skirt was of machine-made cloth, probably the bottom half of a *mother hubbard* that wandering missionaries among the stars liked to clothe their heathen charges in. She had cut off the upper half of the garment, apparently preferring the sunshine and freedom.

Reynolds climbed to the top of the pit and made a half bow, then showed that his hands were empty. (What the devil did you do in a case like this?) The men were carrying what he supposed were gifts: thin shields of beaten copper with crude native designs hammered on them, a few blankets made up of thick furs, and baskets full of freshly slaughtered meat that didn't look at all appetizing.

The men set the gifts on the ground in front of them, then stepped back with malicious smiles on their faces. They chattered for a moment to the girl in their native language.

"These are the challenge gifts of my people, the Mantanai," she intoned ritualistically, her face solemn. "We shall return tomorrow to accept what you give in return."

Reynolds had a feeling that he wasn't supposed to benefit by the gifts.

"What do you mean 'challenge gifts'?" he asked.

She looked like she was going to explain, then changed her mind and gave a short shake to her head.

Reynolds felt the tension build up in him. Her attitude confirmed his opinion that he was going to be in for a difficult time.

The girl turned to leave with the men.

"Wait a minute," Reynolds asked softly. "Is there a Father around?"

She shook her head again and Reynolds thought there was a trace of pity in her eyes.

"No," she said. "The good Father has returned to the skies."

He suspected that she didn't mean the Father had left the planet in the usual manner.

"What happened to him?"

She hesitated a moment and he could feel the slow ooze of sweat on his forehead. Behind her, the other two natives were frowning and shaking their heads with impatience.

"He—he didn't win the game of the Giving of Gifts."

Reynolds cooked his supper over a campfire beside the ship but he had lost most of his appetite and didn't eat much. The gifts from the natives were Greek gifts, he thought. There was something ominous about them, something far different than the friendliness that usually prompted gift giving.

He worried about it for a while, then turned into his crude bed of blankets and air mattress. There was a lot of work to be done the next day, natives or no, and he needed his sleep.

He had just started to doze off when he heard the stealthy footsteps of something moving just beyond the dim circle of light cast by the glowing coals of the fire. The sounds came nearer and he pointed his electric torch in the direction of the quiet rustling and flicked the switch.

The girl stood there, blinded by the glare of the light.

"What do you want?" he asked harshly.

She wet her lips nervously. "The good Father was kind to me," she said, almost in a whisper. "You reminded me of him."

Primitive tribes usually had little regard for their women, he thought, outside of the children they might bear or the work they could do in the fields or in making clothing for the men. The Father's kindnesses had apparently made quite an impression on her.

"What's that got to do with you coming here?"

"I thought that I would tell you about the Giving of Gifts," she said. "I thought that you would like to know."

That was damn sweet of her, he thought cynically—then softened a bit. She was probably running quite a risk in coming to him.

"Tell me about it," he said gently.

She sat down beside him, the light from the coals catching the highlights of her body.

"Father Williams used to say that my people, the Mantanai, were the original capitalists," she started, pronouncing the word uncertainly. "That to us, coppers and furs and grain weren't the means to an end, but an end in itself. That we liked to accumulate wealth merely to play games with it and because it brought—prestige."

She was parroting Father Williams' words, he realized; they meant little to her but she was confident that they meant a lot to him.

"What kind of games?"

She thought for a minute, trying to find a way to

phrase it. "We use our coppers and furs in duels," she said slowly. "Perhaps one chief will give a feast for another and present him with many coppers and blankets. Unless the other chief destroys the gifts and gives a feast in return, at which he presents the first chief with even greater gifts, he loses honor."

He was beginning to see, Reynolds thought. The custom of conspicuous waste, to show how wealthy the possessor was. Enemies dueled with property, instead of with pistols, and the duel would obviously go back and forth until one or the other of its participants was bankrupt—or unwilling to risk more goods. A rather appropriate custom for a planet as lush as this.

"What if one of the chiefs goes broke?" he said, explaining the term.

"If the winning chief demands it, the other can be put to death. He is forced to drink the Last Cup, a poison which turns his bones to jelly. The days go by and he gets weaker and softer until finally he is nothing but a—ball." She described this with a good deal of hand waving and facial animation, which Reynolds found singularly attractive in spite of the gruesomeness of the topic.

"What if a stranger like myself is concerned?"

She looked at him sadly. "Then the pride of the tribe is at stake—and the penalty for losing is always death."

He digested this in silence. "Is that the only way they use their wealth?"

She shook her head. "No. They use it for buying a wife or a house or in paying for a grandson."

She started looking anxiously over her shoulder and he could sense her fear of discovery growing, overcoming her memories of the kindnesses of Father

Williams. He quickly steered the conversation into other channels and found out, among other things, that Father Williams had given her the Christian name of Ruth. He idly wondered what it would have been if Father Williams had been a Buddhist or a Mohammedan. At length, she arose to go.

"You'll come back again some other night, won't you?" Reynolds asked wistfully, suddenly realizing how lonely it was to be in a dangerous situation and have nobody you could talk to.

She hesitated, then flashed him a quick smile and fled into the darkness.

After she had left, Reynolds mused about his position with a sinking heart. They'd be back tomorrow and he'd have to present them with gifts that they considered superior to what they had given him. But he had nothing extra, nothing that he could actually spare.

The only solution—and it was only a stop-gap solution, he realized somberly—was to gradually strip the ship and hope that he had her fixed and ready for flight before the deadly game had reached its climax.

The native representatives and Ruth were back the next day, along with a large crowd of curious onlookers. Reynolds waited inside the ship until they had begun to grow restless, then stepped out carrying his presents.

But there was a ritual to be followed first. He had built a bonfire earlier that morning and he now lighted it. Then he dragged forth the furs and the hampers of meat and the coppers that had been given to him the previous day. He faced the crowd and held up the meat contemptuously, then flung it on the fire. The representatives flushed, but there was an approving murmur from the crowd. The furs he looked at scornfully, then tore the stitches where they had been sewn together and tossed them into the flames. The sheets of beaten copper, which he had previously weakened with acid, he broke into small pieces over his knee and cast them after the furs. The crowd roared approval but Reynolds had no illusion as to their temper. They liked a good "game" but they had no doubt as to what its conclusion would be.

He gestured to Ruth to come over and translate for him to the two red-faced representatives. His voice was loud enough so the crowd could catch the scorn in it, though they didn't understand the words.

"Tell them that the Mantanai bring children's gifts, that they are not fit to accept; that their tribe must indeed be poor if this is all they can afford. Tell them the gifts I shall give them will make theirs look like the castoffs of beggars."

Then he started enumerating his own gifts in turn. One air mattress, two wool blankets, a chair of stainless tubular steel. He hesitated. There wasn't a sound from the crowd, so he continued adding to the pile. A white twill space uniform, a chest of exquisite silver he had meant as a conciliatory gift for his wife, and a set of pale, translucent pottery he had picked up on Altair. The crowd was murmuring now, impressed. Finally, with a show of disdain, he threw on a sleek, black jacket of heavy, shiny leather.

Once again the crowd roared approval, then started to drift away. Ruth nodded slightly; for the moment he had won. But only for the moment.

He worked furiously all afternoon and long into

the night, his welding torch a bright spot of white in the blackness. How much time he had left, he didn't know. But it wouldn't be much.

The next morning he was awakened by the clamor of the crowd outside the rocket. The natives and a sober-faced Ruth were waiting for him, along with a file of men carrying heavy bundles in their arms.

The challenge gifts for the day had arrived.

It was a week since he had crashed on the planet, Reynolds thought jitterily, and despite working practically every waking hour, the job of repairing the ship was still only half done.

And the deadly game had progressed apace.

Everything not absolutely essential to the operation of the ship had gone. Stanchions, railings, ladders—every bit of shiny, glittering metal that he had thought might appeal to the native eyes as being of value. And then all the dishes, the linens, his voco-writer, and most of his clothing had followed. All delivered to the property-crazy natives who had looked them over curiously, then destroyed them to show how worthless the items were in comparison with their own wealth.

And in return, what had he done? How many coppers and furs and blankets had he been forced to destroy? And it meant nothing to the natives because the planet was so lush that there was much, much more where that had come from.

It was the contents of his ship against the resources of a planet and there wasn't the slightest doubt as to how it would turn out.

"I've stripped the ship," he said quietly.

Ruth moved closer to the fire, the yellow light playing on her smooth, tan skin.

"I know," she said. "You've lost the game."

He couldn't have done much better, though, he thought grimly. He had played it out with what he had as well as he could, analyzing the native sense of values so he had some idea of what they attached worth to.

"When will they come for me?" he asked dryly.

She was staring into the fire, the leaping flames reflected in her green eyes.

"Tomorrow, maybe the next day. And then next week you will be nothing but . . ." She left the sentence unfinished and gave an expressive shudder instead.

Reynolds felt a little sick wih fear. There was no way out. If he ran away, he would be running away from his ship and all chance of ever getting home. His chances of surviving alone on the planet would be slim anyways.

"My father will be here tomorrow to watch," Ruth said.

"Your father?"

She showed her teeth. "My father. The chief, the wealthiest man in the village."

They were all turning out, he thought, to watch Reynolds entertain at the big celebration.

Then he caught the look on her face and tried to forget his own troubles. She wasn't having an easy time of it, risking her life to give him information and do what little she could for him.

"How did Father Williams ever get into this mess?" he asked.

"When he first came here," she said, "there was a big sickness. Father Williams helped the Mantanai and my father let him clothe me and teach me your language. But after a few years they forgot and made

Father Williams play the game of the Giving of Gifts."
She paused, and then repeated: "He was very kind to
me."

If he ever got out of it alive, Reynolds thought, he'd
build a monument someplace to the memory of Father Williams.

The clearing around the ship was jammed the next
morning, natives of all shapes and sizes jockeying for
position to see Reynolds' final humbling and open
admittance of the wealth of their tribe. As interested
as brokers on the floor of the stock exchange watching
the quotations on the board, Reynolds thought dryly.
He wondered how some of the natives would do if
they were suddenly transferred to his own society.
With their lust for wealth and shrewdness at manip-
ulating it, they would probably own the universe
within a year.

As usual, he had a bonfire all ready to light. Then
he made a great show at stacking the mounds of coppers and furs and tanned skins and the hampers of
food; probably enough to feed and clothe the village
for a month, he reflected.

"The people of the Mantanai are mighty," he intoned solemnly, Ruth translating, "and their feats at
trapping the *arapai* are sung in hunting songs passed
from father to son." He picked up several of the thick,
luxurious furs lying on one of the piles. "But these
cannot be the pelts of the *arapai;* rather, they are the
thin and smelly hides of the wood rat." And he threw
the pelts scornfully into the flames, following them
up with the others in the stack. The crowd "ohed"
and Reynolds knew the chief's face was burning.

He picked up one of the huge sheets of copper next.

"I have heard tales of the mighty value of the *Copper-of-Many-Suns*, and have heard its praises from many throats. But why then, did you not bring it to me? Why this ugly imitation that would not fool a child of six, this piece of hammered *hunswah*?" He broke it into pieces along the lines etched by acid, and consigned it to the flames. The *Copper-of-the-Autumn-Feast* and the *Copper-of-the-Laughing-Waters* followed.

It was forty minutes later when he had finally thrown the last of the hampers of food into the oily flames, to the approval of the crowd.

Then the chief was striding towards him, magnificent in his richly decorated furs. Ruth trailed after him, her face calm but her eyes showing fright.

"You have destroyed the mighty coppers and the soft skins of the *arapai*," the chief said silkily, "but they were wealth of no great importance. You, perhaps, have gifts that would put these to shame, gifts that will show your might and your own great wealth."

He was faintly sarcastic, knowing full well that Reynolds had stripped his ship.

"I have," Reynolds said calmly, catching the startled look in Ruth's eyes. He pointed to a pile of goods just outside the port of the rocket that he had spent most of the night assembling. "Succulent and tasty foods, breads and meats that will last your tribe for many days, and a machine that will take the basest of materials and turn them into the choicest of delicacies."

The pile included all the provisions he had had on board, including his synthetic food machine.

As before, the crowd good-naturedly shouted their approval and left, knowing that the climax had merely

merely been postponed another day or so.

After they had gone, Reynolds could feel the fingers of fear grip his heart once more. There was no way back now, except the slim chance that Ruth might be able to help him restock on the sly with native foods.

The day was a cloudy one, an excellent day for working on the rocket. The clouds cut the enervating heat of the sun and Reynolds felt filled with a new enthusiasm. Even the odor of burning grease, fired by the heat of his welding torch, smelled good to him. He was a day away from finishing his repairs; another twenty-four hours and he would be on his way to Canopus with an explanation for his delay that was so bizarre it was almost bound to be believed.

He had finished with one of the last strips on a firing tube and was just reaching for another clay-covered welding rod, when he spotted the procession coming down the valley. The chief and the two stern-faced representatives and Ruth. And, as always, the thrill-seeking crowd.

Only twenty-four more hours, he thought agonizedly, and that was to be denied to him! One more turn of the planet's axis and he would have been gone...

"You are to go to my father's house for the next feast," Ruth said heavily. "They are planning it to be the last one."

He dropped his welding torch and made ready to follow Ruth to the village. There was no chance of changing for dinner, he thought grimly, with only one pair of pants left to him. All his other clothing had gone the way of "gifts."

The chief's house was an elaborate, thatched affair

with a large circular opening in the roof. Beneath this opening was the open fireplace, black with the ashes of many fires. Currently there was another fire in it, roasting the huge haunches of meat for the feast and broiling the tubers buried in the coals around its periphery.

The feast was an elaborate one to which, apparently, the entire village had been invited. The enclosure was packed with hot, sweating natives whose eyes were glued on every mouthful of food that Reynolds took and every move he made.

The condemned ate a light meal, Reynolds thought, *and he didn't enjoy a single bite of it.*

The interminable meal and entertainment finally came to a halt and the chief raised his arms for silence. At his signal, a dozen of the young men in the hut disappeared and came back bearing the cartons of supplies and the food machine that had been Reynolds' "gift" a few days before.

"The stranger is mighty," the chief said solemnly, "and has shown that he possesses great wealth. But, alas, his wealth is as nothing to that of the Mantanai." One of the men threw a carton on the flames and Reynolds watched it puff up in smoke. "It is as the dew in the morning, compared to the waters in the ocean." Another carton. "The number of people in this village compare to the blades of grass in the valley."

It was insane, Reynolds thought; a cultural mania that apparently would go to any lengths. A fanatical, perverted capitalism run wild.

The last of the cartons had been consumed in the fire and the food machine reduced to twisted metal when the chief turned to Reynolds.

"It is now our turn to show the might of the Mantanai, the great springs of wealth of our people."

Again the twelve young men disappeared and came back hauling the usual variety of gifts, but this time in an incredible profusion. An exclamation went up from the crowd that quickly dwindled to awed silence as the chief enumerated the gifts.

"The furs of a hundred *arapai*, caught in the prime period of spring, switched and tanned with the gentlest of willow bough . . . the *Copper-of-the-Many-Winters* . . . the *Copper-of-the-Endless-Snows* . . . twenty-two hampers of the plumpest and most perfect of fowls . . . the *Copper-of-the-Wild-Crows* . . . three hampers of the reddest of wood-berries, noted for their succulence and flavor . . ."

The mere enumerating took half an hour and by the time he was finished, the center of the hut was packed with the hampers and furs and the reddish wheels of copper.

The chief finished and turned triumphantly to Reynolds.

"What have you to offer now, stranger? It is your turn for the Giving of Gifts!"

Ruth finished translating by his side and sat down on the floor beside him.

"I have nothing to offer," Reynolds told her in a low voice.

"We are finished then," she said softly.

Now that he had finally reached the climax, Reynolds felt too tired to feel fear. "Say a prayer for me and Father Williams," he said in a dull voice.

She shrugged faintly. "We will say one together."

The way she said it made him glance at her, startled. "What do you mean?"

She laughed softly. "Because we shall be together. They know that I have been helping you. While you have been playing the game, I have been safe. But now that you have lost, whatever happens to you will happen to me."

The crowd was ominously still, waiting for the climactic moment when Reynolds and Ruth would be seized and forced to drink of the Last Cup. The chief was even ready to motion to his aides to seize them, when Reynolds got to his feet and strode to the center of the room.

He stared bitterly at the surprised crowd for a moment, then spat on the nearest copper and hurled it into the fire.

"The gifts of the Mantanai are as the gifts of small children," he said loudly. "The wealth of old women."

He kicked through the assembled gifts like a small cyclone, pulling at the furs and edging the hampers towards the fire, until at last the huge fire had spread to twice its original circumference and the flames had begun to crisp the thatch around the hole in the roof and blister the natives closest to the fire.

When he finally stopped, the crowd was watching him in expectant stillness, waiting for his offer.

"I offer in turn," he said slowly, "a gift of the house of many fires, the arrow of shining metal that voyages among the heavens; my rocket."

There was a roar of astonishment and heads bobbed in eager approval.

He had won again, Reynolds thought weakly, but the comedy was in its last act.

Ruth came to see him early the next morning and they found a secluded spot on the bank of the stream, not far from the now guarded rocket.

"You were very brave," she said.

He resisted an urge to be modest.

"I know."

"My father was very much surprised."

"I rather suspected that he would be," Reynolds said indifferently.

She was quiet for a moment, staring intently into the waters of the stream.

"Will you be sorry not to go back?"

"Of course," he said automatically, then began to give it some thought. Would he be sorry about not going back? If he stayed away, he would be taken for dead and insurance would amply provide for his family. And being provided for was all that they had wanted of him anyway.

Besides, the people here weren't bad people, despite their twisted outlook on matters of property.

"Well, now, I don't know," he added thoughtfully. "Perhaps after a while I could learn to forget..."

She laughed and then asked: "Will you like being a chief?"

He hunched himself up on one elbow and stared at her questioningly. She wasn't smiling any more.

"You will be a chief soon," she said. "At least for several days."

"How do you mean?"

She gestured at the village and the surrounding land. "They will destroy the rocket this afternoon; then all this will be yours as their last gift."

He felt expansive. "That means I've won, then, doesn't it?"

She shook her head. "You will own the village and land, but only for a while."

It was a very clever idea, he thought, suddenly no longer appreciating the beautiful day or Ruth's company. They would give him title to the village and all the lands of the tribe, and there the game would end. Since he was unable to return an even more worthy gift, the remaining portion of the custom would be carried out, during the performance of which he would automatically become an absentee landlord, so to speak, and the property would all revert back to the original owners.

The game was surely at an end. He couldn't very well destroy their "gift" or give them something in return; he was a bankrupt.

He was admiring the landscape and the beautiful stream and the fine tropical weather with a sort of sickly enjoyment, considering it was probably the last time he would be able to do so, when the idea struck him. Why not? What had he to lose?

"How much time have we left, Ruth?"

She looked up at the sun. "Not long, perhaps a few of your hours."

"That's time enough." He grabbed her wrist and then ran downstream, to a small cul-de-sac along the bank, not far from the ship.

The drums of lubricating oil—an even half dozen— were still where he had cached them, to prevent any possible fires when he had been welding on the ship. He found a rock and pounded the spout of one until it broke and the oil was free to gush out, then turned the drum on its side and started rolling it rapidly along the bank, the oil spilling out on the grass and spreading over the calm waters of the stream.

By the time the few hours was up, Reynolds had finished with the last of the drums of oil and was ready to receive the chief and the thrill-seekers from the village.

"The wealth of the Mantanai is great."

(There was a pounding from within the rocket as natives cheerfully hammered the generators and the coils and the delicate thrust machinery with rocks and crude metal bars.)

"The wealth of the Mantanai is as the sands on the beach."

(There was a shaking and rattling sound from the rocket as the delicate meters and instruments were pounded to fragments of glass and metal).

"The wealth of the Mantanai is as boundless as the stars in the heaven."

(There was a hissing noise as the huge bonfire was lit in the control room).

Reynolds watched the destruction of the rocket calmly; he had accepted its ultimate fate for what seemed a long time now. But his turn was coming.

After a long and elaborate ceremony, Reynolds was gifted with the village and the lands surrounding it and presumably the people in it. Then he stepped forward with a lighted torch in his hands.

"The lands of the Mantanai are as the egg of the vulture: worthless. A poor land, with a poor people. See, I think little of it!" and he cast the torch at a wet spot on the ground.

The wet spot flared into flame that became a rapidly twisting snake of fire, leading down to the stream. A moment later, the waters were thick with flames and oily, black smoke.

It looked like Reynolds was indeed bent upon the destruction of the land.

The chief's face was white. "The stranger really means this?"

Reynolds nodded grimly and the first of the drums that he had cached behind the village went up in a roar and a gush of flame. The assembled natives paled. Another drum went up.

"We shall be killed!" the chief cried, his eyes rolling white.

Reynolds smiled. "The property of the Mantanai and the Mantanai themselves are as nothing."

Another drum.

"But you, too, shall die!"

Reynolds shrugged. "My last gift. I knew you wouldn't want to ascend into the skies without taking me along."

The chief suddenly knelt and kissed Reynolds' callused feet. "The wealth of the stranger is mighty; that of the Mantanai is small and insignificant." His face was terror stricken. "The stranger has won the game!"

The last of the drums went up with a loud explosion.

"Perhaps," the chief pleaded, "the wealth of the stranger is so great that he can overlook our own small lands and village?"

They were learning humility at a late date, Reynolds thought. But he nodded solemnly and extended his hands toward the flaming oil barriers around the village. There were no more sudden gushes of flame and gradually the oil on the stream burned out.

He had won, Reynolds thought shakily, won on a bluff with practically no time to spare. Another ten minutes and the flames would have died by themselves, exposing his deception.

But he was still stranded, and stranded now for the

rest of his life. There were compensations, of course, chief among which was the fact that he would be spared his unhappy homecoming on Canopus.

And this planet was comfortable, the weather was nice. And he had always been the comfort-loving sort, anyways.

And then there was Ruth.

"About the girl Ruth," he said to the Chief.

The chief's face immediately grew stern. "She interfered with the game of the Giving of Gifts. She will have to take the Last Cup."

Reynolds was aghast.

"But look here, I own the village and all the lands surrounding it! I . . ."

The chief shook his head. "It is tradition." Then his face grew sly. "But, perhaps if the stranger was willing to consider a gift, the girl could be spared."

There wasn't any doubt as to what he was driving at.

"What do you want?"

Firmly. "The village and lands to revert to their owners."

Later, on the bank of the stream, Ruth leaned her head in the crook of his arm and gazed dreamily at the sky.

"You know why you won, do you not?"

"Certainly. They were afraid they were going to lose all their property."

She shook her head. "Partly. But mostly because you were willing to lose your life, your last gift as you said. They could never have matched it."

He nodded vaguely, not too much interested, and told her his plans for the future and just where she fitted into them. He should have seen long ago, he thought, that her efforts to help him hinged on more than just the past kindnesses of Father Williams.

She didn't reply to his final question.

He flushed, thinking that possibly his conclusions had been all wrong.

"You forget," she said softly. "The bridal price."

He lay back on the bank, his head whirling. With the reversion of the village and lands back to the tribe to save Ruth's life, he was broke. He had no property of his own.

He had won his life—and hers—he thought, but he had finished as a bankrupt in the most brutally capitalistic society that nature had ever created, without even the bridal price for the woman he loved!

Reynolds finished the story, and sipped the last of the wassail in his cup.

"Then when we gave those natives our guns," Harkins said, "it was doing essentially what you had done. Short circuiting the ceremony of the Giving of Gifts by offering our lives, the ultimate gift, the one that couldn't be topped."

"Essentially," Reynolds agreed, "though that's a simplification."

"I don't understand," Jarvis cut in, puzzled. "Harkins here says that the town has been considerably modernized. How was that accomplished?"

Reynolds swirled the last few drops of liquor in his glass and watched the small whirlpool thoughtfully.

"I'm a comfort-loving man myself, and as I became more wealthy and consequently gained more power in the village council, I saw to it that my own ideas for civic improvement were carried out." He started looking around for the wassail bowl. "Quite simple, really."

There was a short silence, leaving an opening for the strains of *Good King Wenceslas* and *Silent Night* emanating from a small group of overly-merry carolers in another corner.

Harkins looked Reynolds slowly up and down and thought to himself that the man was lying like a rug. There were gaps in his story big enough to run the *Churchill* through.

"I was wondering, Mr. Reynolds," he said. "You had to give back the village and lands to save the girl's life." (The way Harkins phrased it, he obviously didn't approve of Reynolds taking up with the native girl, but that was neither here nor there). "And that left you as poor as the proverbial church-mouse. Just how did you gain your wealth and influence?"

"I worked a full year," Reynolds said, "before I earned Ruth's bridal price. Even at that, her bridal price wasn't great, less than that of some of the other belles of the village. (Their tastes in feminine beauty weren't the same as ours, you understand.)"

"I don't quite see what bearing that has on it," Harkins said stiffly.

Reynolds felt around in the folds of his cloak, then passed over a simple drawing to Harkins. It was a crude line drawing of a plump, pleasant-faced woman surrounded by her family.

"I think I told you before, that the natives also used their wealth in paying for their grandsons. That is, a father-in-law would pay a hundred percent interest on the bridal price his daughter's husband had given him on the birth of his first grandson. Two hundred percent for the second child and four hundred percent for the third, doubling each time. Now most of the Mantanai don't care much for many children, but Ruth and I had always thought that we would like a large family. And Ruth's father, you remember, was the wealthiest man in the village."

Harkins was staring open-mouthed at the drawing, counting the number of children and frantically doubling as he went along.

"Of course, a good deal of luck was involved," Reynolds said expansively. "Fifteen children—all boys!"

The Pony

Connie Willis

"Well, aren't you going to open it?" Suzy demanded. Barbara obediently pulled off the red-and-green plaid bow, bracing herself for the twinge of disappointment she always felt when she opened Christmas presents.

"I always just tear the paper, Aunt Barbara," Suzy said. "I picked out this present all by myself. I knew what you wanted from the Macy's parade when your hands got so cold."

Barbara got the package open. Inside was a pair of red-and-purple striped mittens. "It's just what I wanted. Thank you, Suzy," she said. She pointed at the pile of silver boxes under the tree. "One of those is for you, I think."

Suzy dived under the tree and began digging through the presents.

"She really did pick them out all by herself," Ellen whispered, a smile quirking the corners of her mouth.

151

"As you could probably tell by the colors."

Barbara tried on the mittens. I wonder if Joyce got gloves, she thought. At her last session Joyce had told Barbara that her mother always got her gloves, even though she hated gloves and her mother knew it. "I gave one of my patients your phone number," Barbara said to Ellen. "I hope you don't mind."

"Just a little," said her sister. Barbara clenched her mittened fist.

Suzy dumped a silver box with a large blue bow on it in Barbara's lap. "Does this one say, 'To Suzy'?" she asked.

Barbara unfolded the silver card. "It says, 'To Suzy from Aunt Barbara.'" Suzy began tearing at the paper.

"Why don't you open it on the floor?" Ellen said, and Suzy snatched the package off Barbara's lap and dropped to the floor with it.

"I'm really worried about this patient," Barbara said. "She's spending Christmas at home with an unhappy, domineering mother."

"Then why did she go home?"

"Because she's been indoctrinated to believe that Christmas is a wonderful, magical time when everyone is happy and secret wishes can come true," Barbara said bitterly.

"A baseball shirt," Suzy said happily. "I bet now those boys at my preschool will let me play ball with them." She pulled the striped Yankees shirt on over her red nightgown.

"Thank goodness you were able to find the shirt," Ellen said softly. "I don't know what she would have done if she hadn't gotten one. It's all she's talked about for a month."

I don't know what my patient will do either, Barbara thought. Ellen put another red-and-green package in her lap, and she opened it, wondering if Joyce was opening her presents. At Joyce's last session she had talked about how much she hated Christmas morning, how her mother always found fault with all her presents, saying they didn't fit or were the wrong color or that she already had one.

"Your mother's using her presents to express the dissatisfaction she feels with her own life," Barbara had told her. "Of course, everyone feels some disappointment when they open presents. It's because the present is only a symbol for what the person really wants."

"Do you know what I want for Christmas?" Joyce had said as though she hadn't heard a word. "A ruby necklace."

The phone rang. "I hope this isn't your patient," Ellen said, and went into the hall to answer it.

"What does this present say?" Suzy said. She was standing holding another present, a big one with cheap, garish Santa Clauses all over it.

Ellen came back in, smiling. "Just a neighbor calling to wish us a merry Christmas. I was afraid it was your patient."

"So was I," Barbara said. "She's talked herself into believing that she's getting a ruby necklace for Christmas, and I'm very worried about her emotional state when she's disappointed."

"I can't read, you know," Suzy said loudly, and they both laughed. "Does this present say 'To Suzy'?"

"Yes," Ellen said, looking at the tag, which had a Santa Claus on it. "But it doesn't say who it's from. Is this from you, Barbara?"

"It's ominous," Suzy said. "We had ominous presents at my preschool."

"Anonymous," Ellen said, untaping the tag and looking on the back. "They had a gift exchange. I wonder who sent this. Mom's bringing her presents over this afternoon, and Jim decided to wait and give her his when she goes down there next weekend. Go ahead and open it, honey, and when we see what it is, maybe we'll know who it's from." Suzy knelt over the box and started tearing at cheap paper. "Your patient thinks she's getting a ruby necklace?" Ellen said.

"Yes, she saw it in a little shop in the Village, and last week when she went in there again, it was gone. She's convinced someone bought it for her."

"Isn't it possible someone did?"

"Her family lives in Pennsylvania, she has no close friends, and she didn't tell anybody she wanted it."

"Did you buy her the necklace?" Suzy said. She was tearing busily at the Santa Claus paper.

"No," Barbara said to Ellen. "She didn't even tell me about the necklace until after it was gone from the shop, and the last thing I'd want to do would be to encourage her in her mother's neurotic behavior pattern."

"I would buy her the necklace," Suzy said. She had all the paper off and was lifting the lid off a white box. "I would buy it and say, 'Surprise!'"

"Even if she got the necklace, she'd be disappointed in it," Barbara said, feeling obscurely angry at Suzy. "The necklace is only a symbol for a subconscious wish. Everyone has those wishes: to go back to the womb, to kill our mothers and sleep with our fathers, to die. The conscious mind is terrified of those wishes, so it substitutes something safer—a doll or a necklace."

"Do you really think it's that ominous?" Ellen asked, the corners of her mouth quirking again. "Sorry, I'm starting to sound like Suzy. Do you really think it's that serious? Maybe your patient really wants a ruby necklace. Didn't you ever want something really special that you didn't tell anybody about? You did. Don't you remember that year you wanted a pony and you were so disappointed?"

"I remember," Barbara said.

"Oh, it's just what I wanted!" Suzy said so breathlessly that they both looked over at her. Suzy pulled a doll out of a nest of pink tissue and held it out at arm's length. The doll had a pink ruffled dress, yellow curls, and an expression of almost astonishing sweetness. Suzy stared at it as if she were half afraid of it. "It is," she said in a hushed tone. "It's just what I wanted."

"I thought you said she didn't like dolls," Barbara said.

"I thought she didn't. She didn't breathe a word of this." Ellen picked up the box and rustled through the pink tissue paper, looking for a card. "Who on earth do you suppose sent it?"

"I'm going to call her Letitia," Suzy said. "She's hungry. I'm going to go feed her breakfast." She went off into the kitchen, still holding the doll carefully away from her.

"I had no idea she wanted a doll," Ellen said as soon as she was out of sight. "Did she say anything when you took her to Macy's?"

"No," Barbara said, wadding the wrapping paper in her lap into a ball. "We never even went near the dolls. She wanted to look at baseball bats."

"Then how did you know she wanted a doll?"

Barbara stopped with her hands full of paper and plaid ribbon. "I didn't send her the doll," she said angrily. "I bought her the Yankees shirt, remember?"

"Then who sent it to her?"

"How would I know? Jim maybe?"

"No. He's getting her a catcher's mitt."

The phone rang. "I'll get it," Barbara said. She crammed the red paper into a box and went into the hall.

"I just had to call you!" Joyce shouted at her. She sounded nearly hysterical.

"I'm right here," she said soothingly. "I want you to tell me what's upsetting you."

"I'm not upset!" Joyce said. "You don't understand! I got it!"

"The ruby necklace?" Barbara said.

"At first I thought I hadn't gotten it, and I was trying to be cheerful about it even though my mother hated everything I got her and she gave me gloves again; and then, when almost all the presents had been passed out, there it was; in this little box, all wrapped in Santa Claus paper. There was a little tag with a Santa Claus on it, too, and it said, 'To Joyce.' It didn't say who it was from. I opened it, and there it was. It's just what I wanted!"

"Surprise, Aunt Barbara," Suzy said, feeding a cookie shaped like a Santa Claus to her doll.

"I'll wear the necklace to my next session so you can see it," Joyce said, and hung up.

"Barbara," Ellen's voice called from the living room. "I think you'd better come in here."

Barbara took hold of Suzy's hand and walked into

the living room. Ellen was wrestling with a package wrapped in gaudy Santa Claus paper. It was wedged between the Christmas tree and the door. Ellen was behind it, trying to straighten the tree.

"Where did this come from?" Barbara said.

"It came in the mail," Suzy said. She handed Barbara her doll and clambered up on the couch to get to the small tag taped on top.

"There isn't any mail on Christmas," Barbara said.

Ellen squeezed past the tree and around to where Barbara was standing. "I hope it's not a pony," she said, and the corners of her mouth quirked. "It's certainly big enough for one."

Suzy climbed back down, handed Barbara the tag, and took her doll back. Barbara held it a little away from her, as if she were afraid of it. The tag had a Santa Claus on it. It read, "To Barbara." The present was big enough to be a pony. Or something worse. Something only your subconscious knew you wanted. Something too frightening for your conscious mind to even know it wanted.

"It's an ominous present," Suzy said. "Aren't you going to open it?"

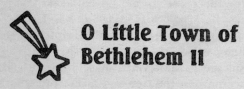

O Little Town of Bethlehem II

Robert F. Young

This morning I take Sandy and Drew into the woods to look for a Christmas tree. The woods are full of them, but finding a good one is difficult, for most of the conifers indigenous to this part of McMullen's Planet lack the natural symmetry of their counterparts on Earth.

Sandy is ten, Drew eight. Christmas Eve is tomorrow night and they can hardly wait for it to come, even though no Santa Claus will come down our chimney. When I reminded them of this, they assured me it made no difference. Christmas this year, they said, will be special enough in itself. In this they are quite right.

Usually when you go into the woods you see some of the Stoops. One of their villages is only a mile from our settlement and the women and children often dig up tubers out of the forest floor. But the woods are

158

empty of them today. No doubt the number of colonists looking for Christmas trees scared them away.

I spot my neighbor, Jake Best. He has his three kids with him and he has just cut down a six-foot "spruce." "Merry Christmas, Glen," he calls out to me.

"Merry Christmas, Jake," I call back.

We find a conifer which is almost pyramidal and just about the right height, and I set to work with my ax. Sandy and Drew insist on carrying it home all by themselves. My wife Melissa meets us at the door. There was a rain last night and she tells us to wipe our feet good before we go in. Our house is a small, square, one-story building without any trimmings, but we are proud of it. Like all the other houses of the settlement and the two churches and the various other buildings, it is build out of plastiwood. Plastiwood, while ideal for setting up a colony in a hurry, isn't a viable building material for cold and windy regions because it's so thin and light, but on this part of McMullen's Planet, winter is barely distinguishable from fall and a close sister to spring, and throughout the year only breezes blow.

After supper I put up the tree in the living room and Melissa and the two kids begin trimming it with strings of popcorn and homemade ornaments. I leave them to their task and head for the square to help trim the big community tree which some of the other colonists and I put up yesterday. The square is in the center of the settlement. It is surfaced with gravel which we hauled in from a nearby creek. We couldn't, of course, bring cement with us because of its weight, and our buildings, unfortunately, lack footings. But we've begun making our own cement, and since it's too late to pour footings, we plan instead to cover the gravel surface of the square with a thick layer of concrete.

The tree is about fifteen feet tall. The children are excited about it and would be running all over the square if Joe Holtz, the mayor, hadn't put it off limits till tomorrow night. Before we put up the tree we affixed the aluminum-foil star, which we brought from Earth, to the peak. We also brought a big box of real ornaments and twenty packages of tinsel and two dozen sets of Christmas tree lights. The Agency for the Development of Extraterrestrial Acres (ADEA) didn't object because the extra weight was negligible.

After we finish trimming the tree, we position the figures of the crèche beside it. ADEA had set up a howl about the crèche, saying we should take something practical instead, but we had the American public on our side and, more importantly, the media. "Of what worth are we to Christianity," a leading commentator demanded, "if we deny to these stalwart colonists, who are going to be present at the first Christmas, the sacred scene which commemorates it?"

When Joe Holtz turns on the tree lights, the tree explodes into multicolored magnificence. The aluminum-foil star seems to shine with a light of its own. We rig up a canopy over the crèche to give the impression of a stable, and Rich Jefferson, the colony's electrician, installs a light under it of much softer radiance than those illuminating the square and which bathes the figures of Mary, Joseph, the shepherds, and the Christ child with a candlelight-like glow. I guess all of us are a bit awed by the effect. The baby Jesus seems to look right up at us out of His crib, ready to bestow His love upon this new world.

To add zest to the occasion we tap a keg of home-made beer. Figured in McMullen time, only a year has passed since our arrival, but a McMullen year equals almost two Earth years, so we've had more than enough time to introduce into our lives some of the daily pleasures we used to take for granted on Earth.

As the beer warms us, a feeling of camaraderie, tinged with self-satisfaction, envelops us. Rich Jefferson puts the way we feel into words when, his black face mirroring the tree lights, he waves his ceramic cup of beer back and forth and says, "We worked hard, men. We worked together, day and night. We came to a strange world and turned it into a new home for mankind. A world so far from Earth it ain't been touched yet with the love of Jesus. We brought some of that love with us. Tomorrow night the rest of it will wash over us like a Wave from heaven." He holds up his cup. All the rest of us hold up ours. "To brotherly love!" he cries, and everyone joins him in the toast.

I leave the square before the others do. I want to get up tomorrow morning with a clear head.

I am thoughtful as I make my way homeward through the narrow streets. The warmth of the beer is still with me and so is the sense of camaraderie.

We named our little colony Bethlehem. I savor the word in my mind. I speak it aloud in the night. "Bethlehem."

Because of the forthcoming miracle, no other name would have done.

I know that in a scientific sense the miracle won't be a true one. It will simply be the result of the forces of nature. Nevertheless, in it, it is possible to find the hand of God.

At 10:16 tomorrow night Christ will be born.

He will be born on Earth, on the third of April, 33 A.D.

It is 2053 light years from Earth to McMullen's Planet. But interstellar ships travel through infraspace where light years do not count, and our journey only lasted a day, ship's time. We traveled back into the past, and although on Earth it is the year of our Lord 2086, were we able to see the planet in our skies, it would be the Earth of 33 A.D.

Early in the twenty-first century time-probes pinpointed the moment of Christ's birth. Before our departure the master computer at Space Base informed us exactly when the wings of light would bring the reality of the event to us. In setting the McMullen date, we chose the traditional rather than the actual month, but moved the day back by one, for Christmas Eve, in the minds of most Christians, has become even holier than Christmas Day.

Although our months are much longer than Earth months, the length of our days is approximately that of Earth days. And, incredibly, the month we have named December is the month when winter in this temperate zone begins!

The Advance Team, which studied the planet and chose the spot where the colony is now located, consists of men and women of diverse religions. Some of them are atheists. After they radioed their report to Earth, they set up their own colony well to the south of the land they had staked out for us. ADEA decided it would be sacrilegious to send any more non-

Christians to a planet that was soon to know the birth of Christ, so for the main colony, equal numbers of Neo-Catholic and Neo-Protestant families were chosen.

We haven't given much thought to Easter. It's too far in our future and some of us may never live to see it. Hopefully those of us who do will be ennobled to an even greater degree when the reality of the resurrection reaches across space and touches our shores.

The next morning Rich Jefferson, Doc Rosario and I set out for the neighboring Stooptown to barter for wild turkeys. The big ship which brought the colonists here stands in a large clearing in the woods just outside the settlement. We walk through its morning shadow. Its rusted hull bespeaks the fact that it is here to stay, just as we are, and will never again see Earth.

In the strict sense of the word, McMullen turkeys aren't true turkeys, but they look enough like them to rate the name, and, when roasted, taste almost the same. Despite their ungainly bodies, they're so fleet of wing none of the colonists has as yet been able to bag one, but the Stoops, using nothing but primitive bows and arrows, bring them down with ease.

In the Stooptown we make our wishes known. By signs, of course, since we can't speak the Stoop language. The Chief, who, like all the members of his race, is bent slightly forward at the waist, summons two of his hunters. We show them the bright-colored pieces of polyester cloth we brought with us and they feel of the material with their dirty fingers and peer at it closely with their sad, brown eyes. The Advance Team classified Stoops as human beings, and despite their awkward posture, they aren't particularly unpleasant to look at, although they're a dirty white in color. Not only are all the adults stooped over, the children are too. Centuries of working in the fields turned what once was an unnatural deformity into a "natural" one.

It might be said that the colonists call the natives "Stoops" because they condemn them. Nothing could be further from the truth. We call them that because the word, logically enough, leaped into our minds the moment we saw them.

After the hunters set forth with their bows and arrows, the Chief asks us about the "Great Tree" that took root in our village and grew lights on its branches. One of the village boys, he "says," saw it from a tree which he climbed in the woods. I know he's lying, that the boy must have sneaked into the colony. This angers me, for Stoop kids are always doing this, and it angers me even more because we'd made our own kids stay home when we trimmed the tree.

I tell him that the tree is an offering which we have made to our God so He will increase the fertility of the women of our tribe, since it would take forever to tell him by signs the real significance of the tree, besides which I'm not altogether certain what the significance is.

While awaiting the return of the hunters we go for a walk through the village. It consists of thatched grass-huts, and there are dozens of ugly little animals running around that look like dogs. Presently we come to the outskirts and look at the fields which, come spring, the Stoops will plow with their wooden plows and then seed, mostly with grain. The soil is dark and rich, and their harvests are phenomenal.

Ironically, our own fields, despite their proximity, consist of a soil comprised mostly of clay, and all we've been able to grow so far with any real degree of success are tomatoes.

"Just think of what we could do," Doc Rosario says, indicating the Stoop fields with a sweeping gesture, "if we had *that* land!"

"Well, we ain't going to get it," Rich says bitterly.

And we aren't. Because the Stoops, having been classified as human beings, have human rights, and ADEA made it clear to us before we left Earth that we could plant only the land which the Advance Team had staked out for us.

I am glad when at length the hunters return. I share Rich's bitterness, as do the rest of the colonists, and it's galling to be exposed to thousands of acres of fertile land which your own countrymen have denied you. The hunters bring back three beautiful birds. We pay for them with our bright pieces of cloth and depart.

Melissa cleans and stuffs our turkey that afternoon. Pastor Rilke pays us a visit while she's still at work. He has decided, he says, to hold midnight services tonight, although it is generally the custom of Neo-Protestant churches to wait till Christmas Day. But since this Christmas Eve will be the first Christmas Eve, he is of the opinion that it would be improper to wait till tomorrow. He has discussed the matter with Father Fardus, he says, and Father Fardus thinks it will be a grand idea for the members of both religions to give their thanks to God at the same time. "I know there's no need to ask you if you'll be present," Pastor Rilke concludes. "I'm merely informing you and the other members of my flock well ahead of time so that our little church will be full."

Sandy asks him if we will be able to feel the Wave of Love when it arrives. He smiles. He is a short, rotund man with a round face. "Yes, Sandy, I think we will. Those of us, that is, who are pure of heart, and I don't think for one moment that any of us are not, especially the little children, of whom He said, or rather of whom He will say, 'Suffer them to come unto me, and forbid them not; for such is the kingdom of God.'"

After he leaves, Sandy and Drew pull the shades in the living room and begin reading a microfilm of "A Christmas Carol." Melissa washes and dries the pots and pans she has dirtied; then she sets about making Christmas cookies. The women's movement, which took such giant steps forward on Earth, has of necessity, here on McMullen's Planet, taken several giant steps backward. Not that the women of the colony have lost their equality—far from it. Someday on our brand new world there will be a wealth of opportunity for the members of both sexes, but at the moment our little settlement has far more in common with the one the Pilgrim Fathers founded in New England than with the ultra-modern world we left behind us, so for the time being, women must do women's work and men men's.

We have a light supper. I have but little appetite and the kids only pick at their food. Melissa leaves more on her plate than she consumes. Since our arrival on McMullen's Planet we have lived for this night. It has made the hardships we have suffered endurable. This is true for all the other colonists.

None of us are "Jesus lovers." Catholics and Protestants alike, we are hard-minded, down-to-earth people. But we are true Christians nevertheless, and we are awed by the thought that tonight our Savior will be born.

Sandy helps Melissa with the dishes. Afterwards the four of us don our best clothes. Best, that is, by our own standards, but to the people of Earth, were any of them around, we would look like farmers as we set out for the square. But neither Melissa nor I would find this offensive, for farmers are what we have become.

The night sky is rich with stars and they seem to have acquired an added brightness. How marvelous it would be if we could see the Star over Bethlehem! But we won't be able to of course, since it won't be a true star, but a syzygy of Jupiter and Saturn.

But it will be in our skies even though we won't be able to see it, and its light will be one with the Wave of Love.

In the square Melissa and I and the kids join the others who are standing around the tree. Its lights have been turned on and glow warmly in the night and the star on its peak shines forth much like the one the Magi will see from the east, even though the light from the syzygy has yet to touch our world. Mary, Joseph and the shepherds gaze down with adoring eyes upon the Infant in the crib.

Pastor Rilke and Father Fardus (who is as tall and thin as Pastor Rilke is short and plump) are standing near the crèche. They join in when we begin singing carols. We fill the night with the words of what for us is the most beloved carol of all—

"O little town of Bethlehem!
How still we see thee lie;
Above thy deep and dreamless sleep
The silent stars go by..."

Many of the people are visibly moved; I glimpse tears in some of the women's eyes. Tears of joy and love.

At 10:15 Father Fardus begins the countdown. Except for his voice, there isn't a sound in the square. "Six...five...four...three...two...one..." All at once a brief brightness illumines the land. Cynics would call it a distant flash of lightning, even though the sky is clear and no sound of thunder reaches our ears, but there are no cynics among us tonight.

Father Fardus and Pastor Rilke kneel. The rest of us follow suit. And so help me, I can *feel* the Wave of Love.

I love my neighbors and I know my neighbors love me. My love reaches out over the land and I feel one with the world we have come to call our own. Around me, both men and women are crying. I feel tears running down my own cheeks.

"Hallelujah!" Pastor Rilke cries. "He is here!" cries Father Fardus. "He is here, He is here, He is here!"

We get to our feet. I see then that three Stoops have come into the square. They make their way through the crowd to the tree. They halt before it, staring up at the star.

No one says a word.

Then the three Stoops go over to the crèche. They stand staring at Mary and Joseph and the shepherds. They look down into the crib. Then one of them kneels before it and places a little bundle on the ground. One of the others reaches into the crib. The silence is broken then. By Father Fardus's voice. "He's touching the Christ child with his filthy hands!"

The priest's horror spreads through the crowd. The horror becomes anger, and then fury. "Drive them away!" Pastor Rilke screams. "Drive them away!"

The gravel covering the square consists of big stones as well as small. I seize one. Men and women scramble for them. One of the Stoops shrieks as a stone glances off his shoulder. They try to make their way out of the square. But the crowd has formed a circle around them.

Pastor Rilke steps over to the crib and kicks away the little bundle as though it were a bomb. It falls apart and tubers tumble over the ground. The air is thick with stones now. The children are throwing them too. One of the Stoops has fallen down. Blood is gushing from his forehead.

"Dirty land hogs!" Henrietta Holtz screams, but the stone she throws goes wild.

Melissa's aim is better. Her stone strikes one of the Stoops on the chest.

"Because of you stupid creeps we have to farm dead land!" Maria Rosario shouts.

"Kill the dirty land hogs!" screams Dorothy Best. "Kill them, kill them, kill them!"

Rich Jefferson picks up a great big stone and heaves it. It misses one of the Stoops by inches. The two who are still on their feet pick up the fallen one. Dragging him, they try to force their way through the crowd. Both are bleeding. The colonists in their path claw at them and strike them with their fists, but they weather the blows and at length they drag their companion off into the darkness. We let them go.

Slowly fury fades from our faces. Love takes its place. The Wave from faraway Earth is still washing over us. Rich Jefferson, who is a soul for neatness, gathers up the scattered tubers, carries them to the edge of the square and throws them into one of the drainage ditches. We begin to sing again. "Silent Night." "Hark! the Herald Angels Sing." "Good King Wenceslas." The voices of adult and child rise heavenward to the stars. Afterward we file into the two churches where Pastor Rilke and Father Fardus give thanks to God for sending us His Son.

The Christmas Present

Gordon R. Dickson

"What is Christmas?" asked Harvey.

"It's the time when they give you presents," Allan Dumay told him. Allan was squatted on his mudshoes, a grubby figure of a little six-year-old boy, in the waning light over the inlet, talking to the Cidorian. "Tonight's Christmas Eve. My daddy cut a thorn tree and my mother's inside now, trimming it."

"Trimming?" echoed the Cidorian. He floated awash in the cool water of the inlet. Someone—perhaps it was Allan's father—had named him Harvey a long time ago. Now nobody called him by any other name.

"That's putting things on the tree," said Allan. "To make it beautiful. Do you know what beautiful is, Harvey?"

"No," said Harvey. "I have never seen beautiful."
But he was wrong—even as, for a different reason,

171

those humans were wrong who called Cidor an ugly swamp-planet because there was nothing green or familiar on the low mud-flats that rose from its planet-wide fresh-water sea—only the stunted, dangerous thorn tree and the trailing weed. There was beauty on Cidor, but it was a different beauty. It was a black-and-silver world where the thorn trees stood up like fine ink sketches against the cloud-torn sky; and this was beautiful. The great and solemn fishes that moved about the uncharted pathways of its seas were beautiful with the beauty of large, far-traveled ships. And even Harvey, though he did not know it himself, was the most beautiful of all with his swelling iridescent jelly-fish body and the yard-long mantle of silver filaments spreading out through it and down through the water. Only his voice was croaky and unbeautiful, for a constricted air-sac is not built for the manufacture of human words.

"You can look at my tree when it's ready," said Allan. "That way you can tell."

"Thank you," said Harvey.

"You wait and see. There'll be colored lights. And bright balls and stars; and presents all wrapped up."

"I would like to see it," said Harvey.

Up the slope of the dyked land that was the edge of the Dumay farm, reclaimed from the sea, the kitchen door of the house opened and a pale, warm finger of light reached out long over the black earth to touch the boy and the Cidorian. A woman stood silhouetted against the light.

"Time to come in, Allan," called his mother's voice.

"I'm coming," he called back.

"Right away! Right now!"

Slowly, he got to his feet.

"If she's got the tree ready, I'll come tell you," he said, to Harvey.

"I will wait," said Harvey.

Allan turned and went slowly up the slope to the house, swinging his small body in the automatic rhythm of the mudshoes. The open doorway waited for him and took him in—into the light and human comfort of the house.

"Take your shoes off," said his mother, "so you don't track mud in."

"Is the tree all ready?" asked Allan, fumbling with the fastenings of his calf-high boots.

"I want you to eat first," said his mother. "Dinner's all ready." She steered him to the table. "Now, don't gulp. There's plenty of time."

"Is Daddy going to be home in time for us to open the presents?"

"You don't open your presents until morning. Daddy'll be back by then. He just had to go upriver to the supply house. He'll start back as soon as it's light; he'll be here before you wake up."

"That's right," said Allan, solemnly, above his plate; "he shouldn't go out on the water at night because that's when the water-bulls come up under your boat and you can't see them in the dark."

"Hush," said his mother, patting him on the shoulder. "There's no water-bulls around here."

"There's water-bulls everywhere. Harvey says so."

"Hush now, and eat your dinner. Your daddy's not going out on the water at night."

Allan hurried with his dinner.

"My plate's clean!" he called at last. "Can I go now?"

"All right," she said. "Put your plate and silverware into the dishwasher."

He gathered up his eating utensils and crammed them into the dishwasher; then ran into the next room. He stopped suddenly, staring at the thorn tree. He could not move—it was as if a huge, cold wave had suddenly risen up to smash into him and wash all the happy warmth out of him. Then he was aware of the sound of his mother's footsteps coming up behind him; and suddenly her arms were around him.

"Oh, honey!" she said, holding him close, "you didn't expect it to be like last year, did you, on the ship that brought us here? They had a real Christmas tree, supplied by the space lines, and real ornaments. We had to just make do with what we had."

Suddenly he was sobbing violently. He turned around and clung to her. "—not a—Christmas tree—" he managed to choke out.

"But, sweetheart, it is!" He felt her hand, soothing the rumpled hair of his head. "It isn't how it looks that makes it a Christmas tree. It's how we think about it, and what it means to us. What makes Christmas is the loving and the giving—not how the Christmas tree looks, or how the presents are wrapped. Don't you know that?"

"But—I—" He was lost in a fresh spate of sobs.

"What, sweetheart?"

"I—promised—Harvey—"

"Hush," she said. "Here—" The violence of his grief was abating. She produced a clean white tissue from the pocket of her apron. "Blow your nose. That's right. Now, what did you promise Harvey?"

"To—" He hiccupped. "To show him a Christmas tree."

"Oh," she said, softly. She rocked him a little in

her arms. "Well, you know honey," she said. "Harvey's a Cidorian; and he's never seen a Christmas tree at all before. So this one would seem just as wonderful to him as that tree on the space ship did to you last Christmas."

He blinked and sniffed and looked at her doubtfully.

"Yes, it would," she assured him gently. "Honey—Cidorians aren't like people. I know Harvey can talk and even make pretty good sense sometimes—but he isn't really like a human person. When you get older, you'll understand that better. His world is out there in the water and everything on land like we have it is a little hard for him to understand."

"Didn't he *ever* know about Christmas?"

"No, he never did."

"Or see a Christmas tree, or get presents?"

"No, dear." She gave him a final hug. "So why don't you go out and get him and let him take a look at the tree. I'll bet he'll think it's beautiful."

"Well . . . all right!" Allan turned and ran suddenly to the kitchen, where he began to climb into his boots.

"Don't forget your jacket," said his mother. "The breeze comes up after the sun goes down."

He struggled into his jacket, snapped on his mudshoes and ran down to the inlet. Harvey was there waiting for him. Allan let the Cidorian climb onto the arm of his jacket and carried the great light bubble of him back into the house.

"See there," he said, after he had taken off his boots with one hand and carried Harvey into the living room. "That's a Christmas tree, Harvey."

Harvey did not answer immediately. He shimmered, balanced in the crook of Allan's elbow, his long filaments spread like silver hair over and around the jacket of the boy.

"It's not a real Christmas tree, Harvey," said Allan. "But that doesn't matter. We have to make do with what we have because what makes Christmas is the loving and the giving. Do you know that?"

"I did not know," said Harvey.

"Well, that's what it is."

"It is beautiful," said Harvey. "A Christmas tree beautiful."

"There, you see," said Allan's mother, who had been standing to one side and watching. "I told you Harvey would think it was beautiful, Allan."

"Well, it'd be more beautiful if we had some real shiny ornaments to put on it, instead of little bits of foil and beads and things. But we don't care about that, Harvey."

"We do not care," said Harvey.

"I think, Allan," said his mother, "you better take Harvey back now. He's not built to be out of the water too long, and there's just time to wrap your presents before bed."

"All right," said Allan. He started for the kitchen, then stopped. "Did you want to say good night to Harvey, Mommy?"

"Good night, Harvey," she said.

"Good night," answered Harvey, in his croaking voice.

Allan dressed and took the Cidorian back to the inlet. When he returned, his mother already had the wrapping papers in all their colors, and the ribbons and boxes laid out on his bed in the bedroom. Also laid out was the pocket whetstone he was giving his father for Christmas and a little inch-and-a-half-high figure he had molded out of native clay, kiln-baked and painted to send home to Allan's grandmother and grandfather, who were his mother's parents. It cost fifty units to ship an ounce of weight back to Earth, and the little figure was just under an ounce—but the grandparents would pay the freight on it from their end. Seeing everything ready, Allan went over to the top drawer of his closet.

"Close your eyes," he said. His mother closed them, tight.

He got out the pair of work gloves he was giving his mother and smuggled them into one of the boxes.

They wrapped the presents together. After they were finished and had put the presents under the thorn tree, with its meager assortment of homemade ornaments, Allan lingered over the wrappings. After a moment, he went to the box that held his toys and got out the container of toy spacemen. They were molded of the same clay as his present to his grandparents. His father had made and fired them, his mother had painted them. They were all in good shape except the astrogator, and his right hand—the one that held the pencil—was broken off. He carried the astrogator over to his mother.

"Let's wrap this, please," he said.

"Why, who's that for?" she asked, looking down at him. He rubbed the broken stump of the astrogator's arm, shyly.

"It's a Christmas present . . . for Harvey."

She gazed at him.

"Your astrogator?" she said. "How'll you run your spaceship without him?"

"Oh, I'll manage," he said.

"But, honey," she said. "Harvey's not like a little

boy. What could he do with the astrogator? He can't very well play with it."

"No," said Allan. "But he could keep it. Couldn't he?"

She smiled, suddenly.

"Yes," she said. "He could keep it. Do you want to wrap it and put it under the tree for him?"

He shook his head, seriously.

"No," he said. "I don't think Harvey can open packages very well. I'll get dressed and take it down to the inlet and give it to him now."

"Not tonight, Allan," his mother said. "It's too late. You should be in bed already. You can take it to him tomorrow."

"Then he won't have it when he wakes up in the morning!"

"All right, then," she said. "I'll take it. But you've got to pop right into bed, now."

"I will." Allan turned to his closet and began to dig out his pajamas. When he was securely established in the warm, blanketing field of the bed, she kissed him and turned out everything but the night light.

"Sleep tight," she said, and taking the broken-armed astrogator, went out of the bedroom, closing the door all but a crack behind her.

She set the dishwasher and turned it on. Then, taking the astrogator again, she put on her own jacket and mudshoes and went down to the shores of the inlet.

"Harvey?" she called.

But Harvey was not in sight. She stood for a moment, looking out over the darkened night country of low-lying earth and water, dimly revealed under the cloud-obscured face of Cidor's nearest moon. A loneliness crept into her from the alien land and she caught herself wishing her husband was home. She shivered a little under her jacket and stooped down to leave the astrogator by the water's edge. She had turned away and was halfway up the slope to the house when she heard Harvey's voice calling her.

She turned about. The Cidorian was at the water's edge—halfway out onto the land, holding wrapped up in his filaments the small shape of the astrogator. She went back down to him, and he slipped gratefully back into the water. He could move on land, but found the labor exhausting.

"You have lost this," he said, lifting up the astrogator.

"No, Harvey," she answered. "It's a Christmas present. From Allan. For you."

He floated where he was without answering, for a long moment. Finally:

"I do not understand," he said.

"I know you don't," she sighed, and smiled a little at the same time. "Christmas just happens to be a time when we all give gifts to each other. It goes a long way back..." Standing there in the dark, she found herself trying to explain; and wondered, listening to the sound of her own voice, that she should feel so much comfort in talking to only Harvey. When she was finished with the story of Christmas and what the reasons were that had moved Allan, she fell silent. And the Cidorian rocked equally silent before her on the dark water, not answering.

"Do you understand?" she asked at last.

"No," said Harvey. "But it is a beautiful."

"Yes," she said, "it's a beautiful, all right." She shivered suddenly, coming back to this chill damp world from the warm country of her childhood. "Harvey," she said suddenly. "What's it like out on the river—and the sea? Is it dangerous?"

"Dangerous?" he echoed.

"I mean with the water-bulls and all. Would one really attack a man in a boat?"

"One will. One will not," said Harvey.

"Now I don't understand you, Harvey."

"At night," said Harvey, "they come up from deep in the water. They are different. One will swim away. One will come up on the land to get you. One will lie still and wait."

She shuddered.

"Why?" she said.

"They are hungry. They are angry," said Harvey. "They are water-bulls. You do not like them?"

She shuddered.

"I'm petrified." She hesitated. "Don't they ever bother you?"

"No. I am . . ." Harvey searched for the word. "Electric."

"Oh." She folded her arms about her, hugging the warmth in to her body. "It's cold," she said. "I'm going in."

In the water, Harvey stirred.

"I would like to give a present," he said. "I will make a present."

Her breath caught a little in her throat.

"Thank you, Harvey," she said, gently and solemnly. "We will be very happy to have you make us a present."

"You are welcome," said Harvey.

Strangely warmed and cheered, she turned and went back up the slope and into the peaceful warmth of the house. Harvey, floating still on the water, watched her go. When at last the door had shut behind her, and all light was out, he turned and moved toward the entrance to the inlet.

It appeared he floated, but actually he was swimming very swiftly. His hundreds of hair-like filaments drove him through the dark water at amazing speed, but without a ripple. Almost, it seemed as if the water was no heavy substance to him but a matter as light as gas through which he traveled on the faintest impulse of a thought. He emerged from the mouth of the inlet and turned upriver, moving with the same ease and swiftness past the little flats and islands. He traveled upriver until he came to a place between two islands where the water was black and deep and the thorn bushes threw their sharp shadows across it in the silver path of the moonlight.

Here he halted. And there rose slowly before him, breaking the smooth surface of the water, a huge and frog-like head, surmounted by two stubby cartilaginous projections above the tiny eyes. The head was as big as an oil drum, but it had come up in perfect silence. It spoke to him in vibrations through the water that Harvey understood.

"Is there a sickness among the shocking people that drives them out of their senses, to make you come here?"

"I have come for beautiful Christmas," said Harvey, "to make you into a present."

It was an hour past dawn the following morning that Chester Dumay, Allan's father, came down the river. The Colony's soil expert was traveling with him and their two boats were tied together, proceeding on a single motor. As they came around the bend between the two islands, they had been talking about an acid condition in the soil of Chester's fields, where they bordered the river. But the soil expert—his name was Père Hama, a lean little dark man—checked himself suddenly in mid-sentence.

"Just a minute—" he said, gazing off and away past Chester Duman's shoulder. "Look at that."

Chester looked, and saw something large and dark floating half-away, caught against the snag of a half-drowned tree that rose up from the muddy bottom of the river some thirty feet out from the far shore. He turned the boat-wheel and drove across toward it.

"What the devil—"

They came up close and Chester cut the motor to let the boats drift in upon the object. The current took them down and the nearer hull bumped against a great black expanse of swollen hide, laced with fragile silver threads and gray-scarred all over by what would appear to have been a fiery whip. It rolled idly in the water.

"A water-bull!" said Hama.

"Is that what it is?" queried Chester, fascinated. "I never saw one."

"I did—at Third Landing. This one's a monster. And *dead!*" There was a note of puzzlement in the soil expert's voice.

Chester poked gingerly at the great carcass and it turned a little. Something like a gray bubble rose to show itself for a second dimly through several feet of murky water, then rolled under out of sight again.

"A Cidorian," said Chester. He whistled. "All crushed. But who'd have thought one of them could take on one of these!" He stared at the water-bull body.

Hama shuddered a little, in spite of the fact that the sun was bright.

"And win—that's the thing," the soil expert said. "Nobody ever suspected—" He broke off suddenly. "What's the matter with you?"

"Oh, we've got one in our inlet that my son plays with a lot—call him Harvey," said Chester. "I was just wondering..."

"I wouldn't let my kid near something that could kill a water-bull," said Hama.

"Oh, Harvey's all right," said Chester. "Still..." Frowning, he picked up the boathook and shoved off from the carcass, turning about to start up the motor again. The hum of its vibration picked up in their ears as they headed downriver once more. "All the same, I think there's no point in mentioning this to the wife and boy—no point in spoiling their Christmas. And later on, when I get a chance to get rid of Harvey quietly..."

"Sure," said Hama. "I won't say a word. No point in it."

They purred away down the river.

Behind them, the water-bull carcass, disturbed, slid free of the waterlogged tree and began to drift downriver. The current swung it and rolled, slowly, over and over until the crushed central body of the dead Cidorian rose into the clean air. And the yellow rays of the clear sunlight gleamed from the glazed pottery countenance of a small toy astrogator, all wrapped about with silver threads, and gilded it.

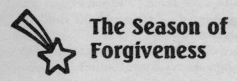

The Season of Forgiveness

Poul Anderson

It was a strange and lonely place for a Christmas celebration—the chill planet of a red dwarf star, away off in the Pleiades region, where half a dozen humans laired in the ruins of a city which had been great five thousand years ago, and everywhere else reached wilderness.

"No!" said Master Trader Thomas Overbeck. "We've got too much work on our hands to go wasting man-hours on a piece of frivolity."

"It isn't, sir," answered his apprentice, Juan Hernández. "On Earth it's important. You have spent your life on the frontier, so perhaps you don't realize this."

Overbeck, a large blond man, reddened. "Seven months here, straight out of school, and you're telling me how to run my shop? If you've learned all the practical technique I have to teach you, why, you

184

may as well go back on the next ship."

Juan hung his head. "I'm sorry, sir. I meant no disrespect."

Standing there, in front of the battered desk, against a window which framed the stark, sullenly lit landscape and a snag of ancient wall, he seemed younger than his sixteen Terrestrial years, slight, dark-haired, big-eyed. The company-issue coverall didn't fit him especially well. But he was quick-witted, Overbeck realized; he had to be, to graduate from the Academy that soon. And he was hard-working, afire with eagerness. The merchants of the League operated over so vast and diverse a territory that promising recruits were always in short supply.

That practical consideration, as well as a touch of sympathy, made the chief growl in a milder tone: "Oh, of course I've no objection to any small religious observance you or the others may want to hold. But as for doing more—" He waved his cigar at the scene outside. "What does it mean, anyway? A date on a chronopiece. A chronopiece adjusted for Earth! Ivanhoe's year is only two-thirds as long; but the globe takes sixty hours to spin around once; and to top it off, this is local summer, even if you don't dare leave the dome unless you're bundled to the ears. You see, Juan, I've got the same right as you to repeat the obvious."

His laughter boomed loud. While the team kept their living quarters heated, they found it easiest to maintain ambient air pressure, a fourth again as high as Terrestrial standard. Sound carried strongly. "Believe it or not," he finished, "I do know something about Christmas traditions, including the very old ones. You want to decorate the place and sing 'Jingle Bells'? That's how to make 'em ridiculous!"

"Please, no, sir," Juan said. "Also on Earth, in the southern hemisphere the feast comes at summer. And nobody is sure what time of year the Nativity really happened." He knotted his fists before he plunged on. "I thought not of myself so much, though I do remember how it is in my home. But that ship will come soon. I'm told small children are aboard. Here will be a new environment for them, perhaps frightening at first. Would we not help them feel easy if we welcomed them with a party like this?"

"Hm." Overbeck sat still a minute, puffing smoke and tugging his chin. His apprentice had a point, he admitted.

Not that he expected the little ones to be anything but a nuisance as far as he himself was concerned. He'd be delighted to leave them behind in a few more months, when his group had ended its task. But part of that task was to set up conditions which would fit the needs of their successors. The sooner those kids adjusted to life here, the sooner the parents could concentrate on their proper business.

And that was vital. Until lately, Ivanhoe had had no more than a supply depot for possible distressed spacecraft. Then a scientific investigator found the *adir* herb in the deserts of another continent. It wouldn't grow outside its own ecology; and it secreted materials which would be valuable starting points for several new organic syntheses. In short, there was money to be gotten. Overbeck's team was assigned to establish a base, make friends with the natives, learn their ways and the ways of their country, and persuade them to harvest the plant in exchange for trade goods.

That seemed fairly well in order now, as nearly as a man could judge amidst foreignness and mystery. The time looked ripe for putting the trade on a regular basis. Humans would not sign a contract to remain for a long stretch unless they could bring their families. Nor would they stay if the families grew unhappy.

And Tom Overbeck wouldn't collect his big, fat bonus until the post had operated successfully for five standard years.

Wherefore the Master Trader shrugged and said, "Well, okay. If it doesn't interfere too much with work, go ahead."

He was surprised at how enthusiastically Ram Gupta, Nikolai Sarychev, Mamoru Noguchi, and Philip Feinberg joined Juan's project. They were likewise young, but not boys; and they had no common faith. Yet together they laughed a lot as they made ready. The rooms and passageways of the dome filled with ornaments cut from foil or sheet metal, twisted together from color-coded wire, assembled from painted paper. Smells of baking cookies filled the air. Men went about whistling immemorial tunes.

Overbeck didn't mind that they were cheerful. That was a boost to efficiency, in these grim surroundings. He argued a while when they wanted to decorate outdoors as well, but presently gave in.

After all, he had a great deal else to think about.

A couple of Ivanhoan days after their talk, he was standing in the open when Juan approached him. The apprentice stopped, waited, and listened, for his chief was in conversation with Raffak.

The dome and sheds of the human base looked

oddly bright, totally out of place. Behind them, the
gray walls of Dahia lifted sheer, ten meters to the
parapets, overtopped by bulbous-battlemented watch-
towers. They were less crumbled than the buildings
within. Today's dwindled population huddled in what
parts of the old stone mansions and temples had not
collapsed into rubble. A few lords maintained small
castles for themselves, a few priests carried on rites
behind porticos whose columns were idols, along
twisting dusty streets. Near the middle of town rose
the former Imperial palace. Quarried for centuries,
its remnants were a colossal shapelessness.

The city dwellers were more quiet than humans.
Not even vendors in their flimsy booths cried their
wares. Most males were clad in leather kilts and weapons, females in zigzag-patterned robes. The wealthy
and the military officers rode on beasts which resembled narrow-snouted, feathery-furred horses. The
emblems of provinces long lost fluttered from the
lances they carried. Wind, shrill in the lanes, bore
sounds of feet, hoofs, groaning cartwheels, an occa-
sional call or the whine of a bone flute.

A human found it cold. His breath smoked into the
dry air. Smells were harsh in his nostrils. The sky
above was deep purple, the sun a dull ruddy disc.
Shadows lay thick; and nothing, in that wan light, had
the same color as it did on Earth.

The deep tones of his language rolled from Raffak's
mouth. "We have made you welcome, we have given
you a place, we have aided you by our labor and
counsel," declared the speaker of the City Elders.

"You have . . . for a generous payment," Overbeck
answered.

"You shall not, in return, exclude Dahia from a full

share in the wealth the *adir* will bring." A four-fingered hand, thumb set oppositely to a man's, gestured outward. Through a cyclopean gateway showed a reach of dusky-green bush, part of the agricultural hinterland. "It is more than a wish to better our lot. You have promised us that. But Dahia was the crown of an empire reaching from sea to sea. Though it lies in wreck, we who live here preserve the memories of our mighty ancestors, and faithfully serve their gods. Shall desert-prowling savages wax rich and strong, while we descendants of their overlords remain weak—until they become able to stamp out this final spark of glory? Never!"

"The nomads claim the wild country," Overbeck said. "No one has disputed that for many centuries."

"Dahia disputes it at last. I came to tell you that we have sent forth emissaries to the Black Tents. They bore our demand that Dahia must share in the *adir* harvest."

Overbeck, and a shocked Juan, regarded the Ivanhoan closely. He seemed bigger, more lionlike than was right. His powerful, long-limbed body would have loomed a full two meters tall did it not slant forward. A tufted tail whipped the bent legs. Mahogany fur turned into a mane around the flat face. That face lacked a nose—breathing was through slits beneath the jaws—but the eyes glowed green and enormous, ears stood erect, teeth gleamed sharp.

The human leader braced himself, as if against the drag of a gravity slightly stronger than Earth's, and stated: "You were foolish. Relations between Dahia and the nomads are touchy at best, violent at worst. Let war break out, and there will be no *adir* trade. Then Dahia too will lose."

"Lose material goods, maybe," Raffak said. "Not honor."

"You have already lost some honor by your action. You knew my people had reached agreement with the nomads. Now you Elders seek to change that agreement before consulting us." Overbeck made a chopping gesture which signified anger and determination. "I insist on meeting with your council."

After an argument, Raffak agreed to this for the next day, and stalked off. Hands jammed into pockets, Overbeck stared after him. "Well, Juan," he sighed, "there's a concrete example for you, of how tricky this business of ours can get."

"Might the tribes really make trouble, sir?" wondered the boy.

"I hope not." Overbeck shook his head. "Though how much do we know, we Earthlings, as short a while as we've been here? Two whole societies, each with its own history, beliefs, laws, customs, desires—in a species that isn't human!"

"What do you suppose will happen?"

"Oh, I'd guess the nomads will refuse flat-out to let the Dahians send gathering parties into their territory. Then I'll have to persuade the Dahians all over again, to let nomads bring the stuff here. That's what happens when you try to make hereditary rivals cooperate."

"Couldn't we base ourselves in the desert?" Juan asked.

"It's better to have a large labor force we can hire at need, one that stays put," Overbeck explained. "Besides, well—" He looked almost embarrassed. "We're after a profit, yes, but not to exploit these poor beings.

An *adir* trade would benefit Dahia too, both from the taxes levied on it and from developing friendlier relations with the tribesfolk. In time, they could start rebuilding their civilization here. It was great once, before its civil wars and the barbarian invasions that followed." He paused. "Don't ever quote me to them."

"Why not, sir? I should think—"

"*You* should. I doubt they would. Both factions are proud and fierce. They might decide they were being patronized, and resent it in a murderous fashion. Or they might get afraid we intend to undermine their martial virtues, or their religions, or something." Overbeck smiled rather grimly. "No, I've worked hard to keep matters simple, on a level where nobody can misunderstand. In native eyes, we Earthlings are tough but fair. We've come to build a trade that will pay off for us, and for no other reason. It's up to them to keep us interested in remaining, which we won't unless they behave. That attitude, that image is clear enough, I hope, for the most alien mind to grasp. They may not love us, but they don't hate us either, and they're willing to do business."

Juan swallowed and found no words.

"What'd you want of me?" Overbeck inquired.

"Permission to go into the hills, sir," the apprentice said. "You know those crystals along Wola Ridge? They'd be beautiful on the Christmas tree." Ardently: "I've finished all my jobs for the time being. It will only take some hours, if I can borrow a flitter."

Overbeck frowned. "When a fight may be brewing? The Black Tents are somewhere that way, last I heard."

"You said, sir, you don't look for violence. Besides, none of the Ivanhoans have a grudge against us. And they respect our power. Don't they? Please!"

"I aim to preserve that state of affairs." Overbeck pondered. "Well, shouldn't be any risk. And, hmm-m-m, a human going out alone might be a pretty good demonstration of confidence. . . . Okay," he decided. "Pack a blaster. If a situation turns ugly, don't hesitate to use it. Not that I believe you'll get in any scrape, or I wouldn't let you go. But—" He shrugged. "There's no such thing as an absolutely safe bet."

Three hundred kilometers north of Dahia, the wilderness was harsh mountainsides, deep-gashed canyons, umber crags, thinly scattered thorn-shrubs and wind-gnarled trees with ragged leaves. Searching for the mineral which cropped here and there out of the sandy ground, Juan soon lost sight of his flitter. He couldn't get lost from it himself. The aircraft was giving off a radio signal, and the transceiver in his pocket included a directional meter for homing on it. Thus he wandered further than he realized before he had collected a bagful.

However slowly Ivanhoe rotates, its days must end. Juan grew aware of how low the dim red sun was, how long and heavy the shadows. Chilliness had turned to a cold which bit at his bare face. Evening breezes snickered in the brush. Somewhere an animal howled. When he passed a rivulet, he saw that it had begun to freeze.

I'm in no trouble, he thought, *but I am hungry, and late for supper, and the boss will be annoyed.* Even now, it was getting hard for him to see. His vision was meant for bright, yellow-white Sol. He stumbled on rocks. Had his radio compass not been luminous-dialed, he would have needed a flashbeam to read it.

Nevertheless he was happy. The very weirdness of this environment made it fascinating; and he could hope to go on to many other worlds. Meanwhile, the Christmas celebration would be a circle of warmth and cheer, a memory of home—his parents, his brother and two sisters, Tío Pepe and Tía Carmen, the dear small Mexican town and the laughter as children struck at a *piñata*—

"*Raielli, Erratan!*"

Halt, Earthling! Juan jarred to a stop.

He was near the bottom of a ravine, which he was crossing as the most direct way to the flitter. The sun lay hidden behind one wall of it, and dusk filled the heavens. He could just make out boulders and bushes, vague in the gloom.

Then metal caught what light there was in a faint glimmer. He saw spearheads and a single breastplate. The rest of the warriors had only leather harness. They were blurs around him, save where their huge eyes gleamed like their steel.

Juan's heart knocked. *These are friends!* he told himself. *The People of the Black Tents are anxious to deal with us—Then why did they wait here for me? Why have a score of them risen out of hiding to ring me in?*

His mouth felt suddenly parched. He forced it to form words, as well as it could imitate the voice of an Ivanhoan. City and wilderness dwellers spoke essentially the same language. "G-greeting." He remembered the desert form of salutation. "I am Juan Sancho's-child, called Hernández, pledged follower of the merchant Thomas William's-child, called Overbeck, and am come in peace."

"I am Tokonnen Undassa's-child, chief of the Elassi Clan," said the lion-being in the cuirass. His tone was a snarl. "We may no longer believe that any Earthling comes in peace."

"What?" cried Juan. Horror smote him. "But we do! How—"

"You camp among the City folk. Now the City demands the right to encroach on our land. . . . Hold! I know what you carry."

Juan had gripped his blaster. The natives growled. Spears drew back, ready to throw. Tokonnen confronted the boy and continued:

"I have heard tell about weapons like yours. A firebeam, fiercer than the sun, springs forth, and rock turns molten where it strikes. Do you think a male of Elassi fears that?" Scornfully: "Draw it if you wish."

Juan did, hardly thinking. He let the energy gun dangle downward in his fingers and exclaimed, "I only came to gather a few crystals—"

"If you slay me," Tokonnen warned, "that will prove otherwise. And you cannot kill more than two or three of us before the spears of the rest have pierced you. We know how feebly your breed sees in the least of shadows."

"But what do you *want*?"

"When we saw you descend, afar off, we knew what we wanted—you, to hold among us until your fellows abandon Dahia."

Half of Juan realized that being kept hostage was most likely a death sentence for him. He couldn't eat Ivanhoan food; it was loaded with proteins poisonous to his kind of life. In fact, without a steady supply of antiallergen, he might not keep breathing. How convince a barbarian herder of that?

The other half pleaded, "You are being wild. What matter if a few City dwellers come out after *adir*? Or

...you can tell them 'no.' Can't you? We, we Earthlings—we had nothing to do with the embassy they sent."

"We dare not suppose you speak truth, you who have come here for gain," Tokonnen replied. "What is our freedom to you, if the enemy offers you a fatter bargain? And we remember, yes, across a hundred generations we remember the Empire. So do they in Dahia. They would restore it, cage us within their rule or drive us into the badlands. Their harvesters would be their spies, the first agents of their conquest. This country is ours. It is strong with the bones of our fathers and rich with the flesh of our mothers. It is too holy for an Imperial foot to tread. You would not understand this, merchant."

"We mean you well," Juan stammered. "We'll give you things—"

Tokonnen's mane lifted haughtily against darkling cliff, twilit sky. From his face, unseen in murk, the words rang: "Do you imagine things matter more to us than our liberty or our land?" Softer: "Yield me your weapon and come along. Tomorrow we will bring a message to your chief."

The warriors trod closer.

There went a flash through Juan. He knew what he could do, must do. Raising the blaster, he fired straight upward.

Cloven air boomed. Ozone stung with a smell of thunderstorms. Blue-white and dazzling, the energy beam lanced toward the earliest stars.

The Ivanhoans yelled. By the radiance, Juan saw them lurch back, drop their spears, clap hands to eyes. He himself could not easily look at that lightning bolt.

They were the brood of a dark world. Such brilliance blinded them.

Juan gulped a breath and ran.

Up the slope! Talus rattled underfoot. Across the hills beyond! Screams of wrath pursued him.

The sun was now altogether down, and night came on apace. It was less black than Earth's, for the giant stars of the Pleiades cluster bloomed everywhere aloft, and the nebula which enveloped them glowed lacy across heaven. Yet often Juan fell across an unseen obstacle. His pulse roared, his lungs were aflame.

It seemed forever before he glimpsed his vehicle. Casting a glance behind, he saw what he had feared, the warriors in pursuit. His shot had not permanently damaged their sight. And surely they tracked him with peripheral vision, ready to look entirely away if he tried another flash.

Longer-legged, born to the planet's gravity, they overhauled him, meter after frantic meter. To him they were barely visible, bounding blacknesses which often disappeared into the deeper gloom around. He could not have hoped to pick them all off before one of them got to range, flung a spear from cover, and struck him.

Somehow, through every terror, he marveled at their bravery.

Run, run.

He had barely enough of a head start. He reeled into the hull, dogged the door shut, and heard missiles clatter on metal. Then for a while he knew nothing.

When awareness came back, he spent a minute giving thanks. Afterward he dragged himself to the pilot chair. *What a scene!* passed across his mind. And, a crazy chuckle: *The old definition of adventure. Somebody else having a hard time a long ways off.*

He slumped into the seat. The vitryl port showed him a sky turned wonderful, a land of dim slopes and sharp ridges—He gasped and sat upright. The Ivan-hoans were still outside.

They stood leaning on their useless spears or cling-ing to the hilts of their useless swords, and waited for whatever he would do. Shakily, he switched on the sound amplifier and bullhorn. His voice boomed over them: "What do you want?"

Tokonnen's answer remained prideful. "We wish to know your desire, Earthling. For in you we have met a thing most strange."

Bewildered, Juan could merely respond with, "How so?"

"You rendered us helpless," Tokonnen said. "Why did you not at once kill us? Instead, you chose to flee. You must have known we would recover and come after you. Why did you take the unneeded risk?"

"You *were* helpless," Juan blurted. "I couldn't have . . . hurt you . . . especially at this time of year."

Tokonnen showed astonishment. "Time of year? What has that to do with it?"

"Christmas—" Juan paused. Strength and clarity of mind were returning to him. "You don't know about that. It's a season which, well, commemorates one who came to us Earthlings, ages ago, and spoke of peace as well as much else. For us, this is a holy time." He laid hands on controls. "No matter. I only ask you believe that we don't mean you any harm. Stand aside. I am about to raise this wagon."

"No," Tokonnen said. "Wait. I ask you, wait." He was silent for a while, and his warriors with him.

"What you have told us—We must hear further. Talk to us, Earthling."

Once he had radioed that he was safe, they stopped worrying about Juan at the base. For the next several hours, the men continued their jobs. It was impossible for them to function on a sixty-hour day, and nobody tried. Midnight had not come when they knocked off. Recreation followed. For four of them, this meant preparing their Christmas welcome to the ship.

As they worked outdoors, more and more Dahians gathered, fascinated, to stand silently around the plaza and watch. Overbeck stepped forth to observe the natives in his turn. Nothing like this had ever happened before.

A tree had been erected on the flagstones. Its sparse branches and stiff foilage did not suggest an evergreen; but no matter, it glittered with homemade ornaments and lights improvised from electronic parts. Before it stood a manger scene that Juan had constructed. A risen moon, the mighty Pleiades, and the luminous nebular veil cast frost-cold brilliance. The beings who encompassed the square, beneath lean houses and fortress towers, formed a shadow-mass wherein eyes glimmered.

Feinberg and Gupta decorated. Noguchi and Sarychev, who had the best voices, rehearsed. Breath from their song puffed white.

"O little town of Bethlehem,
How still we see thee lie—"

A muted "A-a-ahhh!" rose from the Dahians, and Juan landed his flitter.

He bounded forth. Behind him came a native in a steel breastplate. Overbeck had awaited this since the boy's last call. He gestured to Raffak, speaker of the Elders. Together, human and Ivanhoan advanced to greet human and Ivanhoan.

Tokonnen said, "It may be we misjudged your intent, City folk. The Earthling tells me we did."

"And his lord tells me we of Dahia pushed forward too strongly," Raffak answered. "That may likewise be."

Tokonnen touched sword-hilt and warned, "We shall yield nothing which is sacred to us."

"Nor we," said Raffak. "But surely our two people can reach an agreement. The Earthlings can help us make terms."

"They should have special wisdom, now in the season of their Prince of Peace."

"Aye. My fellows and I have begun some hard thinking about that."

"How do you know of it?"

"We were curious as to why the Earthlings were making beauty, here where we can see it away from the dreadful heat," Raffak said. "We asked. In the course of this, they told us somewhat of happenings in the desert, which the far-speaker had informed them of."

"It is indeed something to think about," Tokonnen nodded. "They, who believe in peace, are more powerful than us."

"And it was war which destroyed the Empire. But come," Raffak invited. "Tonight be my guest. Tomorrow we will talk."

They departed. Meanwhile the men clustered around Juan. Overbeck shook his hand again and again. "You're a genius," he said. "I ought to take lessons from you."

"No, please, sir," his apprentice protested. "The thing simply happened."

"It wouldn't have, if I'd been the one who got caught."

Sarychev was puzzled. "I don't quite see what did go on," he confessed. "It was good of Juan to run away from those nomads, instead of cutting them down when he had the chance. However, that by itself can't have turned them meek and mild."

"Oh, no." Overbeck chuckled. His cigar end waxed and waned like a variable star. "They're as ornery as ever—same as humans." Soberly: "The difference is, they've become willing to listen to us. They can take our ideas seriously, and believe we'll be honest brokers, who can mediate their quarrels."

"Why could they not before?"

"My fault, I'm afraid. I wasn't allowing for a certain part of Ivanhoan nature. I should have seen. After all, it's part of human nature too."

"What is?" Gupta asked.

"The need for—" Overbeck broke off. "You tell him, Juan. You were the one who did see the truth."

The boy drew breath. "Not at first," he said. "I only found I could not bring myself to kill. Is Christmas not when we should be quickest to forgive our enemies? I told them so. Then . . . when suddenly their whole attitude changed . . . I guessed what the reason must be." He searched for words. "They knew—both Dahians and nomads knew—we are strong; we have powers they can't hope to match. That doesn't frighten them. They have to be fearless, to survive in as bleak a country as this.

"Also, they have to be dedicated. To keep going through endless hardship, they must believe in something greater than themselves, like the Imperial dream of Dahia or the freedom of the desert. They're ready to die for those ideals.

"We came, we Earthlings. We offered them a fair, profitable bargain. But nothing else. We seemed to have no other motive than material gain. They could not understand this. It made us too peculiar. They could never really trust us.

"Now that they know we have our own sacrednesses, well, they see we are not so different from them, and they'll heed our advice."

Juan uttered an unsteady laugh. "What a long lecture, no?" he ended. "I'm very tired and hungry. Please, may I go get something to eat and afterward to bed?"

As he crossed the square, the carol followed him:

"—The hopes and fears of all the years
Are met in thee tonight."

Christmas without Rodney

Isaac Asimov

It all started with Gracie (my wife of nearly forty years) wanting to give Rodney time off for the holiday season and it ended with me in an absolutely impossible situation. I'll tell you about it if you don't mind because I've got to tell *somebody*. Naturally, I'm changing names and details for our own protection.

It was just a couple of months ago, mid-December, and Gracie said to me, "Why don't we give Rodney time off for the holiday season? Why shouldn't he celebrate Christmas, too?"

I remember I had my optics unfocused at the time (there's a certain amount of relief in letting things go hazy when you want to rest or just listen to music) but I focused them quickly to see if Gracie were smiling or had a twinkle in her eye. Not that she has much of a sense of humor, you understand.

She wasn't smiling. No twinkle. I said, "Why on

202

Earth should we give him time off?"

"Why not?"

"Do you want to give the freezer a vacation, the sterilizer, the holoviewer? Shall we just turn off the power supply?"

"Come, Howard," she said. "Rodney isn't a freezer or a sterilizer. He's a *person*."

"He's not a person. He's a robot. He wouldn't want a vacation."

"How do you know? And he's a *person*. He deserves a chance to rest and just revel in the holiday atmosphere."

I wasn't going to argue that "person" thing with her. I know you've all read those polls which show that women are three times as likely to resent and fear robots as men are. Perhaps that's because robots tend to do what was once called, in the bad old days, "women's work" and women fear being made useless, though I should think they'd be delighted. In any case, Gracie *is* delighted and she simply adores Rodney. (That's *her* word for it. Every other day she says, "I just adore Rodney.")

You've got to understand that Rodney is an old-fashioned robot whom we've had about seven years. He's been adjusted to fit in with our old-fashioned house and our old-fashioned ways and I'm rather pleased with him myself. Sometimes I wonder about getting one of those slick, modern jobs, which are automated to death, like the one our son, DeLancey, has, but Gracie would never stand for it.

But then I thought of DeLancey and I said, "How are we going to give Rodney time off, Gracie? DeLancey is coming in with that gorgeous wife of his" (I was using "gorgeous" in a sarcastic sense, but Gracie didn't notice—it's amazing how she insists on seeing a good side even when it doesn't exist) "and how are we going to have the house in good shape and meals made and all the rest of it without Rodney?"

"But that's just it," she said, earnestly. "DeLancey and Hortense could bring *their* robot and he could do it all. You *know* they don't think much of Rodney, and they'd love to show what theirs can do and Rodney can have a rest."

I grunted and said, "If it will make you happy, I suppose we can do it. It'll only be for three days. But I don't want Rodney thinking he'll get every holiday off."

It was another joke, of course, but Gracie just said, very earnestly, "No, Howard, I will talk to him and explain it's only just once in a while."

She can't quite understand that Rodney is controlled by the three laws of robotics and that nothing has to be explained to him.

So I had to wait for DeLancey and Hortense, and my heart was heavy. DeLancey is my son, of course, but he's one of your upwardly mobile, bottom-line individuals. He married Hortense because she has excellent connections in business and can help him in that upward shove. At least, I hope so, because if she has another virtue I have never discovered it.

They showed up with their robot two days before Christmas. The robot was as glitzy as Hortense and looked almost as hard. He was polished to a high gloss and there was none of Rodney's clumping. Hortense's robot (I'm sure she dictated the design) moved absolutely silently. He kept showing up behind me for no reason and giving me heart-failure every time I turned around and bumped into him.

Worse, DeLancey brought eight-year-old LeRoy. Now he's my grandson, and I would swear to Hortense's fidelity because I'm sure no one would voluntarily touch her, but I've got to admit that putting him through a concrete mixer would improve him no end.

He came in demanding to know if we had sent Rodney to the metal-reclamation unit yet. (He called it the "bust-up place.") Hortense sniffed and said, "Since we have a modern robot with us, I hope you keep Rodney out of sight."

I said nothing, but Gracie said, "Certainly, dear. In fact, we've given Rodney time off."

DeLancey made a face but didn't say anything. He knew his mother.

I said, pacifically, "Suppose we start off by having Rambo make something good to drink, eh? Coffee, tea, hot chocolate, a bit of brandy—"

Rambo was their robot's name. I don't know why except that it starts with R. There's no law about it, but you've probably noticed for yourself that almost every robot has a name beginning with R. R for robot, I suppose. The usual name is Robert. There must be a million robot Roberts in the northeast corridor alone.

And frankly, it's my opinion that's the reason human names just don't start with R any more. You get Bob and Dick but not Robert or Richard. You get Posy and Trudy, but not Rose or Ruth. Sometimes you get unusual R's. I know of three robots called Rutabaga, and two that are Rameses. But Hortense is the only one I know who named a robot Rambo, a syllable-combination I've never encountered, and I've never liked to ask why. I was sure the explanation would prove to be unpleasant.

Rambo turned out to be useless at once. He was, of course, programmed for the DeLancey/Hortense menage and that was utterly modern and utterly automated. To prepare drinks in his own home, all Rambo had to do was to press appropriate buttons. (Why anyone would need a robot to press buttons, I would like to have explained to me!)

He said so. He turned to Hortense and said in a voice like honey (it wasn't Rodney's city-boy voice with its trace of Brooklyn), "The equipment is lacking, madam."

And Hortense drew a sharp breath. "You mean you *still* don't have a robotized kitchen, grandfather?" (She called me nothing at all, until LeRoy was born, howling of course, and then she promptly called me "grandfather." Naturally, she never called me Howard. That would tend to show me to be human, or, more unlikely, show *her* to be human.)

I said, "Well, it's robotized when Rodney is in it."

"I dare say," she said. "But we're not living in the twentieth century, grandfather."

I thought: How I wish we were—but I just said, "Well, why not instruct Rambo how to operate the controls. I'm sure he can pour and mix and heat and do whatever else is necessary."

"I'm sure he can," said Hortense, "but thank Fate he doesn't have to. I'm not going to interfere with his programming. It will make him less efficient."

Gracie said, worried, but amiable, "But if we don't interfere with his programming, then I'll just have to instruct him, step by step, but I don't know how it's done. I've never done it."

I said, "Rodney can tell him."

Gracie said, "Oh, Howard, we've given Rodney a vacation."

"I know, but we're not going to ask him to *do* anything; just tell Rambo here what to do and then Rambo can do it."

Whereupon Rambo said stiffly, "Madam, there is nothing in my programming or in my instructions that would make it mandatory for me to accept orders given me by another robot, especially one that is an earlier model."

Hortense said, soothingly, "Of course, Rambo. I'm sure that grandfather and grandmother understand that." (I noticed that DeLancey never said a word. I wonder if he *ever* said a word when his dear wife was present.)

I said, "All right, I tell you what. I'll have Rodney tell *me*, and then I will tell Rambo."

Rambo said nothing to that. Even Rambo is subject to the second law of robotics which makes it mandatory for him to obey human orders.

Hortense's eyes narrowed and I knew that she would like to tell me that Rambo was far too fine a robot to be ordered about by the likes of me, but some distant and rudimentary near-human waft of feeling kept her from doing so.

Little LeRoy was hampered by no such quasi-human restraints. He said, "I don't want to have to look at Rodney's ugly puss. I bet he don't know how to do *anything* and if he does, ol' Grampa would get it all wrong anyway."

It would have been nice, I thought, if I could be alone with little LeRoy for five minutes and reason calmly with him, with a brick, but a mother's instinct told Hortense never to leave LeRoy alone with any human being whatever.

There was nothing to do, really, but get Rodney out of his niche in the closet where he had been enjoying his own thoughts (I wonder if a robot has his own thoughts when he is alone) and put him to work. It was hard. He would say a phrase, then I would say the same phrase, then Rambo would do something, then Rodney would say another phrase and so on.

It all took twice as long as if Rodney were doing it himself and it wore *me* out, I can tell you, because everything had to be like that, using the dishwasher/sterilizer, cooking the Christmas feast, cleaning up messes on the table or on the floor, everything.

Gracie kept moaning that Rodney's vacation was being ruined, but she never seemed to notice that mine was, too, though I *did* admire Hortense for her manner of saying something unpleasant at every moment that some statement seemed called for. I noticed, particularly, that she never repeated herself once. Anyone can be nasty, but to be unfailingly creative in one's nastiness filled me with a perverse desire to applaud now and then.

But, really, the worst thing of all came on Christmas Eve. The tree had been put up and I was exhausted. We didn't have the kind of situation in which an automated box of ornaments was plugged into an electronic tree, and at the touch of one button there would result an instantaneous and perfect distribution of ornaments. On our tree (of ordinary, old-fashioned plastic) the ornaments had to be placed, one by one, by hand.

Hortense looked revolted, but I said, "Actually,

Hortense, this means you can be creative and make your own arrangement."

Hortense sniffed, rather like the scrape of claws on a rough plaster wall, and left the room with an obvious expression of nausea on her face. I bowed in the direction of her retreating back, glad to see her go, and then began the tedious task of listening to Rodney's instructions and passing them on to Rambo.

When it was over, I decided to rest my aching feet and mind by sitting in a chair in a far and rather dim corner of the room. I had hardly folded my aching body into the chair when little LeRoy entered. He didn't see me, I suppose, or he might simply have ignored me as being part of the less important and interesting pieces of furniture in the room.

He cast a disdainful look on the tree and said, to Rambo, "Listen, where are the Christmas presents? I'll bet old Gramps and Gram got me lousy ones, but I ain't going to wait for no tomorrow morning."

Rambo said, "I do not know where they are, Little Master."

"Huh!" said LeRoy, turning to Rodney. "How about you, Stink-face. Do you know where the presents are?"

Rodney would have been within the bounds of his programming to have refused to answer on the grounds that he did not know he was being addressed, since his name was Rodney and not Stink-face. I'm quite certain that would have been Rambo's attitude. Rodney, however, was of different stuff. He answered politely, "Yes, I do, Little Master."

"So where is it, you old puke?"

Rodney said, "I don't think it would be wise to tell you, Little Master. That would disappoint Gracie and

Howard who would like to give the presents to you tomorrow morning."

"Listen," said little LeRoy, "who you think you're talking to, you dumb robot? Now I gave you an order. You bring those presents to me." And in an attempt to show Rodney who was master, he kicked the robot in the shin.

It was a mistake. I saw it would be that a second before and that was a joyous second. Little LeRoy, after all, was ready for bed (though I doubted that he ever went to bed before he was *good* and ready). Therefore, he was wearing slippers. What's more, the slipper sailed off the foot with which he kicked, so that he ended by slamming his bare toes hard against the solid chrome-steel of the robotic shin.

He fell to the floor howling and in rushed his mother. "What is it, LeRoy? What is it?"

Whereupon little LeRoy had the immortal gall to say, "He hit me. That old monster-robot *hit* me."

Hortense screamed. She saw me and shouted, "That robot of yours must be destroyed."

I said, "Come, Hortense. A robot can't hit a boy. First law of robotics prevents it."

"It's an *old* robot, a *broken* robot. LeRoy says—"

"LeRoy lies. There is no robot, no matter how old or how broken, who could hit a boy."

"Then *he* did it. *Grampa* did it," howled LeRoy.

"I wish I did," I said, quietly, "but no robot would have allowed me to. Ask your own. Ask Rambo if he would have remained motionless while either Rodney or I had hit your boy. Rambo!"

I put it in the imperative, and Rambo said, "I would not have allowed any harm to come to the Little Master, Madam, but I did not know what he purposed.

He kicked Rodney's shin with his bare foot, Madam."

Hortense gasped and her eyes bulged in fury. "Then he had a good reason to do so. I'll still have your robot destroyed."

"Go ahead, Hortense. Unless you're willing to ruin your robot's efficiency by trying to reprogram him to lie, he will bear witness to just what preceded the kick and so, of course, with pleasure, will I."

Hortense left the next morning, carrying the pale-faced LeRoy with her (it turned out he had broken a toe—nothing he didn't deserve) and an endlessly wordless DeLancey.

Gracie wrung her hands and implored them to stay, but I watched them leave without emotion. No, that's a lie. I watched them leave with lots of emotion, all pleasant.

Later, I said to Rodney, when Gracie was not present, "I'm sorry, Rodney. That was a horrible Christmas, all because we tried to have it without you. We'll never do that again, I promise."

"Thank you, Sir," said Rodney. "I must admit that there were times these two days when I earnestly wished the laws of robotics did not exist."

I grinned and nodded my head, but that night I woke up out of a sound sleep and began to worry. I've been worrying ever since.

I admit that Rodney was greatly tried, but a robot *can't* wish the laws of robotics did not exist. He *can't*, no matter what the circumstances.

If I report this, Rodney will undoubtedly be scrapped, and if we're issued a new robot as recompense, Gracie will simply never forgive me. Never! No robot, however new, however talented, can possibly replace Rodney in her affection.

In fact, I'll never forgive myself. Quite apart from my own liking for Rodney, I couldn't bear to give Hortense the satisfaction.

But if I do nothing, I live with a robot capable of wishing the laws of robotics did not exist. From wishing they did not exist to acting as if they did not exist is just a step. At what moment will he take that step and in what form will he show that he has done so?

What do I do? What do I do?

Christmas Treason

James White

Richard sat on the woolly rug beside his brother's cot and watched the gang arrive one by one.

Liam came first wearing a thick sweater over pajamas too tight for him—his parents didn't have central heating. Then Mub, whose folks did not need it, in a nightie. When Greg arrived he fell over a truck belonging to Buster, because he was coming from the daytime, and the moonlight coming into the room was too dim for him to see properly. The noise he made did not disturb the sleeping grownups, but Buster got excited and started rattling the bars of his cot and had to be shushed. Loo arrived last, with one of her long, funny dresses on, and stood blinking for a while, then sat on the side of Richard's bed with the others.

Now the meeting could begin.

For some reason Richard felt worried even though the Investigation was going fine, and he hoped this

213

was just a sign that he was growing up. His Daddy and the other big people worried nearly all the time. Richard was six.

"Before hearing your reports," he began formally, "we will have the Minutes of the last—"

"Do we *hafta*...?" whispered Liam angrily. Beside him Greg said a lot of nonsense words, louder than a whisper, which meant the same thing. Mub, Loo and his three-year-old brother merely radiated impatience.

"*Quiet!*" Richard whispered, then went on silently, "There has got to be Minutes, that book of my Daddy's says so. And talk without making a noise, I can hear you just as well...."

That was his only talent, Richard thought enviously. Compared with the things the others could do it wasn't much. He wasn't able to go to Loo's place, with its funny shed that had no sides and just a turned up roof, or play pirates on the boat Liam's Daddy had given him. There was a big hole in the boat and the engine had been taken out, but there was rope and nets and bits of iron in it, and sometimes the waves came so close it seemed to be floating. Some of the gang were frightened when the big waves turned white and rushed at them along the sand, but *he* wouldn't have been scared if he had been able to go there. Nor had he been to Mub's place, which was noisy and crowded and not very nice, or climbed the trees beside Greg's farm.

Richard couldn't go *anywhere* unless a grown-up took him in a train or a car or something. Whereas if the others wanted to go somewhere they just went— even Buster could do it now. All he could do was listen and watch through their minds when they were playing and, if one of them wanted to say something complicated to the others, he would take what they were thinking and repeat it so everybody could hear it. And it was only his friends' minds he could get into—if only he could see what *Daddy* was thinking!

He was the oldest and the leader of the gang, but by itself that wasn't much fun....

"I want my train set!" Greg broke in impatiently. A bright but indistinct picture of the promised model railway filled Richard's mind, to be overlaid rapidly by pictures of Mub's dolly, Loo's blackboard, Liam's cowboy suit and Buster's machine-gun. His head felt like bursting.

"Stop thinking so loud!" Richard ordered sharply. "You'll get them, you'll all get them. We were promised."

"I know, but..." began Greg.

"...How?" ended the others, in unison.

"That's what the Investigation is for, to find out," Richard replied crossly. "And we'll never find out if you keep rushing things. Quiet, gang, and listen!"

The room was already silent and then even the thinking noises died down. Richard began to speak in a whisper—he had found that talking while he was thinking kept his mind from wandering onto something else. And besides, he had learned some new grown-up words and wanted to impress the gang with them.

He said, "Two weeks ago Daddy asked Buster and me what we wanted for Christmas and told us about Santa. Santa Claus will bring you anything you want. Or any two things, or even three things, within reason, my Daddy says. Buster doesn't remember last Christmas, but the rest of us do and that's the way it happens.

You hang up your stocking and in the morning there's sweets and apples and things in it, and the *big* stuff you asked for is on the bed. But the grown-ups don't seem to know for sure how they got there..."

"S-sleigh and reindeer," Greg whispered excitedly.

Richard shook his head. "None of the grown-ups can say how exactly it happens, they just tell us that Santa will come all right, that we'll get our toys in time and not to worry about it. But we can't help worrying about it. That's why we're having an Investigation to find out what really happens.

"We can't see how one man, even when he has a sleigh and magic reindeer that fly through the air, can bring everybody their toys all in one night..." Richard took a deep breath and got ready to use his new, grown-up words. "Delivering all that stuff during the course of a single night is a logistical impossibility."

Buster, Mub and Greg looked impressed. Loo thought primly, "Richard is showing off," and Liam said, "I think he's got a jet."

Feeling annoyed at the mixed reception to his big words, Richard was getting ready to whisper "Yah, Slanty-Eyes!" at Loo when he thought better of it and said instead, "Jets make a noise and we'd remember if we heard one last Christmas. But what we're supposed to do in an Investigation is get the facts and then find the answer—" he glared at Loo—"by a process of deductive reasoning."

Loo didn't say or think a word.

"All right then," Richard went on briskly, "this is what we know..."

His name was Santa Claus. Description: a man, big even for a grown-up, fresh complexion, blue eyes, white hair and beard. He dressed in a red cap, coat and trousers, all trimmed with white fur, also black shiny belt and knee-boots. Careful questioning of grown-ups showed that they were all in agreement about his appearance, although none of them had admitted to actually seeing him. Liam's Daddy had been questioned closely on this point and had said that he knew because Liam's Grandad had told *him*. It was also generally agreed that he lived somewhere at the North Pole in a secret cavern under the ice. The cavern was said to contain his toy workshops and storage warehouses.

They knew quite a lot about Santa. The major gap in their knowledge was his methods of distribution. On Christmas Eve, did he have to shoot back and forth to the North Pole when he needed his sleigh refilled? If so it was a very chancy way of doing things and the gang had good cause to be worried. They didn't want any hitches on Christmas Eve, like toys coming late or getting mixed up. If anything they wanted them to come early.

Two weeks ago Richard had seen his mother packing some of his old toys in a box. She had told him that they were going to the orphans because Santa never came to orphans.

The gang had to be *sure* everything would be all right. Imagine wakening on Christmas morning to find you were an *orphan!*

". . . We can't get any more information at this end," Richard continued, "so we have to find the secret cavern and then see how he sends the stuff out. That was your last assignment, gang, and I'll take your reports now.

"You first, Mub."

Mub shook her head, she had nothing to report. But there was a background picture of her Daddy's face looking angry and shiny and sort of loose, and a smack from her Daddy's large, pink-palmed hand which had hurt her dignity much more than her bottom. Sometimes her Daddy would play with her for hours and she could ask him questions all the time, but other times he would come into the house talking funny and bumping into things the way Buster had done when he was just learning to walk, and then he would smack her if she asked questions all the time. Mub didn't know what to make of her Daddy sometimes.

Still without a word she floated up from the bed and drifted to the window. She began staring out at the cold, moonlit desert and the distant buildings where Richard's Daddy worked.

"Loo?" said Richard.

She had nothing to report either.

"Liam."

"I'll wait to last," said Liam smugly. It was plain that he knew something important, but he was thinking about seagulls to stop Richard from seeing what it was.

"All right, Greg then."

"I found where some of the toys are stored," Greg began. He went on to describe a trip with his mother and father into town to places called shops, and two of them had been full of toys. Then when he was home again his father gave him a beating and sent him to bed without his supper...

"O-o-oh," said Loo and Mub sympathetically.

This was because, Greg explained, he had seen a dinky little tractor with rubber treads on it that could climb over piles of books and things. When he got home he thought about it a lot, and then thought that he would try reaching for it the way they all did when they were somewhere and had left things they wanted to play with somewhere else. His Daddy had found him playing with it and smacked him, four times with his pants down, and told him it was wrong to take things that didn't belong to him and that the tractor was going right back to the shop.

But the beating had only hurt him for a short time and he was nearly asleep when his mother came and gave him a hug and three big chocolates with cream in the middle. He had just finished eating them when his father brought in some more . . .

"O-h-h," said Loo and Mub, enviously.

"Feeties for *me?*" asked Buster, aloud. When excited he was apt to slip back into baby talk. Greg whispered "Night"—a nonsense word he used when he was thinking "No"—and added silently, "I ate them all."

"Getting back to the Investigation," Richard said firmly, "Dad took Buster and me to a shop the day before yesterday. I've been to town before but this time I was able to ask questions, and this is the way they work. Everybody doesn't always know exactly what they want for Christmas, so the stores are meant to show what toys Santa has in stock so they'll know what to ask for. But the toys in the shops can't be touched until Christmas, just like the ones at the North Pole. Daddy said so, and when we were talking to Santa he said the same thing . . ."

"*Santa!!!*"

A little awkwardly Richard went on, "Yes, Buster and I spoke to Santa. We . . . I asked him about his sleigh and reindeer, and then about what seemed to us to be a logistically insoluble problem of supply and distribution. When we were asking him he kept looking at Daddy and Daddy kept looking up in the air, and that was when we saw his beard was held on with elastic.

"When we told him about this," Richard continued, "he said we were very bright youngsters and he had to admit that he was only one of Santa's deputies in disguise, sent to say Merry Christmas to all the boys and girls because Santa himself was so rushed with toy-making. He said that Santa didn't even tell *him* how he worked the trick, it was a Top Secret, but he did know that Santa had lots of computers and things and that the old boy believed in keeping right up to date science-wise. So we didn't have to worry about our toys coming, all that would be taken care of, he said.

"He was a very nice man," Richard concluded, "and didn't mind when we spotted his disguise and asked all the questions. He even gave us a couple of small presents on account."

As he finished Richard couldn't help wondering if that deputy had told everything he knew—he had looked very uncomfortable during some of the questions. Richard thought that it was a great pity that he couldn't listen to what everybody was thinking instead of just the kids in his gang. If only they knew where that secret cavern was.

"I know," said Liam suddenly. "I found it."

Everybody was asking questions at once then, and they were talking instead of just thinking. Where was it and had he seen Santa and was my train-set there and what were the toys like . . . ? In his mind Richard thundered, "Quiet! You'll wake my Daddy! And I'll ask the questions." To Liam he said, "That's great! How did you find it?"

One of Liam's abilities—one shared by Greg and Buster, and to a lesser degree by the girls—was of thinking about a place he would like to be and then going there. Or to be more precise, going to one of the places that were most like the place he wanted to go. He did not think of where so much as what he wanted—a matter of environment rather than geography. He would decide whether the place should have night, day, rain, sunshine, snow, trees, grass or sand and then think about the fine details. When his mental picture was complete he would go there, or they all—with the exception of Richard—would go there. Liam and Greg had found lots of lovely places in this way, which the gang used when they grew tired of playing in each other's backyards, because once they went to a place they always knew how to go back to it.

This time Liam had been trying for ice caverns with toys and reindeer stalls in them and had got nowhere at all. Apparently no such place existed. Then he started asking himself what would a place look like if it had to make and store things, and maybe had to send them out to people fast. The answer was machinery. It mightn't be as noisy or dirty as the factory his Daddy had taken him to in Derry last summer, but there would have to be machinery.

But there might not be toys—they might not have been made or arrived yet. And if, as Richard had suggested, reindeer and sleighs were no longer in use, then they were out of the picture as well. And the ice cavern, now, that would be a cold place for Santa to work and if he turned on a heater the walls would melt, so the cavern might not be made of ice. What he was left with was a large underground factory or storehouse either at or somewhere near the North Pole.

It wasn't a very good description of the place he was looking for, but he found it.

In Liam's mind was the memory of a vast, echoing corridor so big it looked like a street. It was clean and brightly lit and empty. There was a sort of crane running along the roof with grabs hanging down, a bit like the ones he had seen lifting coal at the docks only these were painted red and yellow, and on both sides of the corridor stood a line of tall, splendid, unmistakable shapes. Rockets.

Rockets, thought Richard excitedly: *that was the answer, all right!* Rockets were faster than anything, although he didn't quite see how the toys would be delivered. Still they would find that out easily now that they knew where the secret cavern was.

"Did you look inside them for toys?" Greg broke in, just ahead of the others asking the same question.

Liam had. Most of the rockets were filled with machinery and the nose had sort of sparkly stuff in it. All the ones he had looked at were the same and he had grown tired of floating about among the noses of the rockets and gone exploring instead. At the other end of the corridor there was a big notice with funny writing on it. He was standing in front of it when two grown-ups with guns started running at him and yelling nonsense words. He got scared and left.

When Liam finished, the girls began congratulating him and the hole in the chest of his sweater grew bigger. Then Greg tried to cut him down to size again by stating, "They weren't nonsense words. What the guards yelled at you, I mean. If you could remember better how they sounded I could tell you what they said . . ."

Just when things were getting exciting, Richard thought impatiently, another argument was going to start about what were nonsense words and what weren't. Buster, Liam and himself could make themselves understood to each other whether they were speaking or thinking, but when any of the others spoke aloud it was just nonsense. And they said the same thing about words Richard, Liam and Buster spoke aloud. But the funny thing was that Loo, Mub and Greg couldn't understand what each other said, either.

Richard had an idea that this was because they lived in different places, like in the pictures he had studied in his Daddy's *National Geographic* magazines. He had tracked down Liam's place from some of those pictures—Liam lived in a fishing village on the North Irish coast. Why they spoke a funny, but recognizable, form of American there Richard didn't know. Loo and Mub were harder to pin down; there were a couple of places where the people had slanty eyes or had dark brown skin and black curly hair. Greg was the hardest because he didn't have any special skin or hair or eyes. His folks wore furry hats in winter, but that wasn't much to go on . . .

"What do we do now, Richard?" Liam broke in. "Keep thinking about the cavern, huh? Not your Daddy's old books."

For a moment Richard thought into himself, then he opened his mind and asked, "How much time have you all got?"

Mub said it was near her dinner-time. Greg had just finished breakfast and was supposed to be playing in the shed for the next three or four hours. Loo's time was about the same as Greg's. Liam thought it was nearly breakfast time, but his mother didn't mind if he stayed in bed these cold mornings. And Buster, like Richard, had practically the whole of the night to play around in.

"Right," he said briskly when all the reports were in. "It looks like the cavern Liam found isn't the right one—the rockets don't have toys in them. Maybe it's a place for sending toys out, but they haven't arrived from Santa's workshop yet. That workshop is the place we're looking for, and it shouldn't be hard to find now that we know the sort of place to look for—an underground place with rockets."

His thoughts became authoritative as he went on. "You've got to find these underground places and see what goes on in them. We can't be sure of anything we've been told about them, so there might be a lot of secret caverns. When you find one try not to let anybody see you, look around for toys and see if you can get to the office of the man in charge of the place. If it's Santa or he looks like a nice man, ask him questions. And remember to say please and thank you. If he's not a nice man, or if there's nobody there, try to find out things whatever way you can. Everyone understand?"

Everybody thought, "Yes."

"Okay then. Greg will go to the cavern Liam found, because he can understand what the people say there. Liam and Buster will look for caverns on their own. But remember, once you see that a place doesn't have toys in it, leave and look somewhere else. Don't waste time. Mub and Loo will stay here and be ready to help if you need them, they can't go to new places as easily as you men can."

Richard's mouth felt suddenly dry. He ended, "All right, take off."

Buster flicked out of sight in the middle of a "Wheee-e-e" of excitement. Liam held back for a moment thinking, "But why do they have guards in the caverns?" To which Greg replied, "Maybe to protect the toys against juvenile delinquents. I don't know what they are exactly, but my Daddy says they steal and break things, and if I had kept that tractor I took from the shop I would grow up to be one." Then Liam and Greg quietly disappeared. Loo and Mub began gathering up Buster's teddybear and toys. They floated into Buster's cot with them and started to play houses.

Richard got into bed and lay back on his elbows. Buster was the member of the gang most likely to get into trouble so he listened in for him first. But his brother was in a place where each rocket was held out level by a little crane instead of standing straight up. The sound of voices and footsteps echoed about the place in a spooky fashion, but his brother had not been spotted. Buster reported that he had looked into the noses of the rockets and they were filled with a lot of junk and some stuff which sparkled and frightened him away.

The stuff didn't sparkle really, of course, but Buster had a talent for looking through things—like brick walls and engine casings—and when he looked into the rocket nose in that way the stuff sparkled. Like the electric wiring at home, he thought, only worse. There were no toys or any sign of Santa, so he was going to try some other place. Richard switched to Greg.

Greg was in the cavern originally found by Liam. Two of the guards were still talking about seeing a boy in pajamas. Greg was going to look around some more and then try another place. Liam's report was much the same, right down to the stuff in the rocket noses which made him afraid to go too close. Richard stopped listening to them and began thinking to himself.

Why had the caverns guards in them? To protect the toys against damage or theft, as Greg had suggested? But where were the toys? The answer to that question was, some of them were in the shops . . .

A bit of conversation between his mother and father, overheard yesterday when they were in one of the shops, popped suddenly into his mind. Richard hadn't known exactly what was going on because he had been watching to see that Buster didn't knock over anything. Daddy had asked his mother if she would like something—beads or a shiny brooch or something—for Christmas. Mummy had said, "Oh John, it's lovely but . . ." Then a man from behind the counter had come up to Daddy, said a few words and gone away again. Daddy had said, "Okay." Then Mummy had said, "But John, are you sure you can afford it? It's robbery, sheer robbery! These store-keepers are robbers at Christmas time!"

Guards all over the place, Greg's theory, and store-keepers who were robbers at Christmas time. It was beginning to make sense, but Richard was very worried by the picture that was forming.

Loo and Mub had the cot pillow and the teddybear floating in the air above the cot, with Buster's broken truck doing a figure-of-eight between them. But they were being careful not to make a noise so Richard did not say anything. He began listening in for the others again.

Buster had found another cavern, so had Liam. Greg had gone through three more—they had all been small places and plainly not what the gang was looking for. All reported rockets with the same puzzling load, no sign of toys and no Santa. And so it went on. Richard's eyes began to feel heavy and he had to sit on the edge of the bed again to keep from falling asleep.

Mub was lying in Buster's cot being a sick Mummy and Loo was kneeling beside her being the Nurse. At the same time they had taken the truck apart and now a long procession of parts was in orbit around the pillow and teddybear. Richard knew they would put the truck together again before they went home, and probably fix it, too. He wished that he could do something useful like that, and he began to wonder if Loo could move people, too.

When he mentioned the idea to her she stopped being a Nurse long enough to do some experiments. Richard tried as hard as he could to stay sitting on the edge of his bed, but Loo forced him to lie flat on his back. It was as if a big, soft cushion was pushing against his arms and chest. When he tried to prop his elbows behind him, other cushions pushed his arms out straight. After he had been forced to lie flat three times, Loo told him she wanted to go back to playing Nurse. She didn't like this other game because it made her head hurt.

Richard went back to listening to the searchers again.

Buster was working on his fourth cavern, Liam and Greg on their seventh and ninth respectively. The sudden speeding up of the search was explained by the fact that they no longer walked from place to place inside the caverns, they just *went.* Tired legs, Richard discovered, had been the reason for them all thinking of this time-saving idea. It seemed to get the guards all excited, though. Everywhere the gang went there were guards who got excited—it was hard to stay hidden with so many guards about—but they had not stayed anywhere long enough to be caught. They had found lots of rockets but no sign of a toy workshop, or Santa.

Richard was now pretty sure that the guards were soldiers. In some of the caverns they wore dark green uniforms with black belts and red things on their shoulders, and only Greg could understand the nonsense words they said. In another place, the cavern Liam had searched where you could hear planes taking off, they'd had blue-gray uniforms with shiny buttons and rings on their sleeves and Liam had been able to understand them. Then in a lot of other caverns they had been dressed like that picture of Daddy downstairs, taken when he had been working in a place called Korea.

But where was *Santa*?

During the next three hours the search still failed to reveal his whereabouts. Mub went home for her breakfast and Loo for her dinner, both with orders to come back tomorrow night or sooner if Richard called them. Liam had another two hours before his mother expected him out of bed. Greg had to break off for dinner.

But he was back to searching caverns again within

half an hour, and it was then that Richard noticed something funny about the reports that were coming back. It was as if he was seeing the same caverns twice—the same red-painted cranes, the same groupings of rockets, even the same guards' faces. The only explanation he could think of was that caverns were being searched which had been searched before.

Quickly he told the gang of his suspicions and opened his mind to receive and relay. This meant that Buster, Greg and Liam knew everything that was in each other's minds having to do with the search, including the total number of caverns found up to that time together with their identifying characteristics. Knowing this they would no longer be in danger of going over ground already searched by another member of the gang. Richard then told them to go looking for new caverns.

They tried, and couldn't find one.

Altogether they had uncovered forty-seven of them, from *big* underground places with hundreds of rockets in them down to small places with just a few. And now it seemed plain that this was all the caverns there were, and there was *still* no trace of Santa Claus.

"We've missed something, gang," Richard told them worriedly. "You've got to go back to the biggest caverns again and look around some more. This time ask questions—"

"B-but the guards run at you and yell," Greg broke in. "They're not nice men."

"No," Liam joined in, "they're scary."

Buster said, "I'm hungry."

Richard ignored him and said, "Search the big caverns again. Look for important places, places where there are lots of guards. Find the boss and ask *him* questions. And don't forget to say please and thank you. Grown-ups will give you practically anything if you say please...."

For a long time after that nothing happened. Richard kept most of his attention on Buster, because his brother had a tendency to forget what he was looking for if anything interesting turned up. Buster was becoming very hungry and a little bored.

His next contact with Liam showed the other hiding behind a large metal cabinet and looking out at a big room. Three walls of the room were covered from floor to ceiling with other cabinets, some of which made clicking, whirring noises and had colored lights on them. The room was empty now except for a guard at the door, but it had not always been that way. In Liam's mind Richard could see the memory of two men in the room who had talked and then left again before Liam could ask them questions. They had been wearing blue-gray uniforms and one of them had had gold stuff on his cap. Liam had remembered every word they said, even the long ones which he didn't understand.

The cabinets with the flashing lights on them were called a Director-Computer, and it worked out speeds and Tradge Ectories so that every rocket in this cavern, and in about twenty others just like it, would be sent to the spot it was meant to go and hit it right on the button. It would tell hundreds and hundreds of rockets where to go, and it would send them off as soon as there was a blip. Liam didn't know what a blip was, however. Did Richard?

"No," said Richard impatiently. "Why didn't you ask one of the guards?"

Because the man with the gold stuff on his cap had

told the guard that the situation was getting worse, that there were reports from all over of bases being Infil Trated, and that some sort of Halloo Sinatory weapon was being used because the guards had insisted that the saboteurs were not adults. He had said trust them to play a dirty trick like this just before Christmas, and he had told the guard to kill any unauthorized personnel trying to enter the computer room on sight. Liam didn't know what an unauthorized personnel was, but he thought it might mean him. And anyway, he was hungry and his mother would be expecting him down from bed soon and he wanted to go home.

"Oh, all right," said Richard.

Maybe it was a sleigh and reindeer he used in Daddy's young days, he thought excitedly, *but* now it is rockets. And computers *to tell them where to go, just like the deputy Santa told us!*

But why were the guards being told to kill people? Even unauthorized personnel—which sounded like a very nasty sort of people, like juvenile delinquents maybe. Who was pulling what dirty trick just before Christmas? And where were the toys? In short, who was lousing up his and everyone else's Christmas?

The answer was becoming clearer in Richard's mind, and it made him feel mad enough to hit somebody. He thought of contacting Greg, then decided that he should try to find out if he could fix things instead of just finding out more about what had gone wrong. So he called up Loo and Mub, linked them to each other through his mind, and spoke:

"Loo, do you know the catapult Greg keeps under his mattress? Can you send it here without having to go to Greg's place to look for it?"

The grubby, well-used weapon was lying on Richard's bed.

"Good," he said. "Now can you send it b—"

The catapult was gone.

Loo wasn't doing anything special just then and wouldn't have minded continuing with the game. But it wasn't a game to Richard, it was a test.

"Mub, can you do the same?"

Mub's Daddy was at work and her mother was baking. Mub was waiting to lick the spoon with the icing sugar on it. A little absently she replied, "Yes, Richard."

"Does it make your heads tired?" he asked anxiously.

Apparently it didn't. The girls explained that it was hard to make people, or pussycats, or goldfish move because live things had minds which kind of pushed back, but dead things didn't have anything to push back with and could be moved easily. Richard told them thanks, broke away, then made contact with Greg.

Through Greg's eyes and mind he saw a large desk and two men in dark green uniforms behind it—one standing behind the other, an older and bigger man who was sitting down. Greg was in a chair beside the desk and only a few feet away from the bigger man.

"Your name is Gregor Ivanovitch Krejinski," said the big man, smiling. He was a nice big man, a little like Greg's Daddy, with dark gray hair and lines at the corners of his eyes. He looked like he was scared of Greg but was trying to be nice anyway. Greg, and through him the watching Richard, wondered why he should be scared.

"And you say your parents have a farm not far from

a town," the big man went on gently. "But there are no farms or towns such as you describe within three hundred miles of here. What do you say to that, Little Gregor?

"Now suppose you tell me how you got here, eh?"

That was a difficult question. Greg and the other members of the gang didn't know how they got to places, they just went.

"I just . . . came, sir," said Greg.

The man who was standing lifted his cap and rubbed his forehead, which was sweating. In a low voice he spoke to the big man about other launching bases which had been similarly penetrated. He said that relations with the other side had been almost friendly this past year or so, but it was now obvious that they had been lulled into a sense of false security. In his opinion they were being attacked by a brand new psychological weapon and all firing officers should be ready with their finger on the big red button ready for the first blip. The big man frowned at him and he stopped talking.

"Well, now," the big man resumed to Greg, "if you can't say how you came, can you tell me why, Gregor?"

The big man was sweating now, too.

"To find Santa Claus," said Greg.

The other man began to laugh in a funny way until the big man shushed him and told him to phone the Colonel, and told him what to say. In the big man's opinion the boy himself was not a threat but the circumstances of his appearance here were cause for the gravest concern. He therefore suggested that the base be prepared for a full emergency launch and that the Colonel use his influence to urge that all other bases be similarly prepared. He did not yet know what tactic was being used against them, but he would continue with the interrogation.

"Now, son," he said, returning to Greg, "I can't tell you how to find Santa Claus exactly, but maybe we could do a trade. You tell me what you know and I'll tell you what I know."

Richard thought the big man was very nice and he told Greg to find out all he could from him, then he broke away. It was time he checked on Buster again.

His brother was just on the point of revealing himself to a man sitting in a small room with lots of colored lights around the walls. There was a big glass screen on one wall with a white line going round and round on it, and the man was bent forward in his chair, holding his knees tightly with his hands. He was chewing.

"Feeties...?" asked Buster hopefully.

The man swung round. One hand went to the gun at his belt and the other shot out to stop with one finger on a big red button on his panel, but he didn't push it. He stared at Buster with his face white and shiny and his mouth open. There was a little piece of chewing gum showing on his teeth.

Buster was disappointed; he had thought the man might have been eating cakes of toffee. Chewing gum wasn't much good when you were *hungry*. Still, maybe if he was polite the man might give him some anyway, and even tell him where Santa Claus was.

"How do'oo doe," he said carefully.

"F-fine thanks," said the man, and shook his head. He took his finger off the big red button and pushed another one. He began talking to somebody:

"Unauthorized person in the Firing...No, no, I don't have to push the button...I know the orders, dammit, but this is a kid! About three, w-wearing pajamas. . . . "

A few minutes later two men ran in. One was thin and young and he told the man at the panel to keep his blasted eyes on the screen in case there was a blip instead of gawking at the kid. The other one was big and broad and very like the man who had asked Greg questions—except he had on a tie instead of a high, tight collar. The second man looked at Buster for a long time, then got down on one knee.

"What are you doing here, sonny?" he said in a funny voice.

"Looking for Santa," said Buster, looking at the man's pockets. They looked empty, not even a hanky in them. Then, on Richard's prompting, he added, "What's a . . . a blip?"

The man who was standing began to speak rapidly. He said that this was some sort of diversion, that guards at bases all over had been reporting kids, that the other side was working up to some sort of sneak punch. And just when everybody thought relations were improving, too. Maybe this wasn't a kid, maybe this was a child impersonator . . .

"Impersonating a three-year-old?" asked the big man, straightening up again.

All the talk had not helped Richard much and he was getting impatient. He thought for a minute, then made Buster say, "What's a blip . . . *please!*"

The big man went to the one who was sitting in front of the screen. They whispered together, then he walked toward Buster.

"Maybe we should T-I-E his H-A-N-D-S," said the thin man.

In a quiet voice the big man said, "Contact the General. Tell him that until further notice I consider it advisable that all launching bases be placed in Condition Red. Meanwhile I'll see what I can find out. And call Doc, we might as well check on your child impersonation theory."

He turned away from the now open locker with a candy bar in his hand, stripping off the wrapping as he added, "Don't they teach you psychology these days?" And to Buster he said, "A blip is a teeny white mark on a screen like that man is watching."

Buster's mind was so full of thinking about the candy bar that it was hard for Richard to make him ask the proper questions. *Ask him what* makes *a blip?* he thought furiously at his brother—why were the minds of grown-ups impossible to get into!—and eventually he got through.

"A rocket going up," said the big man; then added crossly, "This is ridiculous!"

"What makes a rocket go up?" prompted Richard.

The man who was watching for blips was holding his knees tightly again. Nobody was talking to him but he said, "One way is to push a big red button . . ." His voice sounded very hoarse.

Watching and listening through his brother's mind Richard decided that he had heard and seen enough. For some time he had been worried about the safety of Greg and Liam and Buster—all the talk of shooting, and the way the guards looked so cross at just a few children who weren't doing any harm. Richard had seen people get shot lots of times on television, and while he hadn't thought much about what being dead meant, getting shot had looked like a very sore thing. He didn't want it happening to any of his gang, especially now when he was sure that there was no reason to go on with the search.

Santa had hid out somewhere, and if what Richard suspected was true, he couldn't blame him. *Poor Santa,* he thought.

Quickly Richard called off the search. He thought he knew what was going on now, but he wanted to think about it some more before deciding what to do. Almost before he had finished Buster was back in his cot, still working on the candy bar. Richard made his brother give him half of it, then he got into bed himself. But not to sleep.

Mub and Loo had never seen any of the caverns yet so he had to attend to that chore first. Using the data available in the three boys' minds he was able to direct the girls to all forty-seven places with no trouble at all. The girls were seen a couple of times but nothing happened—they were just looking, not asking questions. When he was sure they understood what they had to do Richard let them go home, but told them to start practicing on rocks and things outside his window. After that he lay on his side and looked out at the moonlit desert.

Small rocks and big boulders began to move about. They arranged themselves into circles and squares and stars, or built themselves into cairns. But mostly they just changed places with each other too fast for Richard to see. Fence posts disappeared leaving the wire sagging but unbroken and bushes rose into the air with the ground undisturbed beneath them and every root intact. After an hour of it Richard told them to stop and asked them if they were *sure* it didn't make their heads tired.

They told him no, that moving dead things was easy.

"But you'll have to work awful fast ..." Richard began.

Apparently it didn't matter. Just so long as they knew where everything was they could move it just like *that*, and Mub sent a thought of her Daddy snapping his fingers. Relieved, Richard told them to put everything out on the desert back the way it had been and to start getting to know the other places he had told them about. They went off joyfully to mix the gang's business with their own pleasure.

Richard became aware of movements downstairs. It was nearly breakfast time.

Since the early hours of the morning Richard had been sure he knew what had gone wrong with the Christmas business, and the steps the gang must take to put matters right again—or as near right as it was possible to put them. It was a terrific responsibility for a six-year-old, and the trouble was that he hadn't heard the grown-ups' side of it. What he intended doing could get him into bad trouble if his Daddy found out—he might even get beaten. Richard's parents had taught him to respect other people's property.

But his Daddy was usually a bit dopey at breakfast time. Maybe he would be able to ask some questions without his Daddy asking too many back.

"Daddy," he said as he was finishing his cereal, "d'you know all those rockets Santa has in his secret caverns at the North Pole? And the stuff in the nose of them that you're not allowed to go near ... ?"

His Daddy choked and got cross and began talking to his mother. He said that he would never have taken this out-of-the-way job if he hadn't been sure that Richard's mother, being an ex-schoolteacher, could look after the children's education. But it was quite obvious that she was forcing Richard far too much and he was too young to be told about things like rocket bases. To which his mother replied that his Daddy didn't believe her when she told him that Richard could read the *National Geographic*—and not just pretend to read them—and even an odd whodunit. Sure she had taught him more than a normal six-year-old but that was because he could take it—she wasn't doing a doting mother act, Richard really was an exceptionally bright boy. And *she* hadn't told him about rocket bases, he must have got it from a magazine or something...

And so it went on. Richard sighed, thinking that every time he asked a complicated question his mother and father started arguing about him between themselves and ignoring his question completely.

"Daddy," said Richard during a lull, "they're big people's toys, aren't they?"

"Yes!" his father snapped. "But the big people don't want to play with them. In fact, we'd be better off without them!" Then he turned and went back to arguing with their mother. Richard excused himself and left, thinking at Buster to follow him as soon as he could.

So the big people didn't want their toys, Richard thought with grim satisfaction. That meant the gang was free to go ahead.

All that day Richard listened in on Loo and Mub. The girls were fast but there was an awful lot to do so he set Greg and Liam to helping them—the boys could move things, too, but not as fast as the girls. But everybody had been awake for so long they began to fall asleep one by one. When it happened to Buster and Richard their mother thought they were taking sick and was worried, but both of them were up as fresh as ever when their father came home so she didn't mention it. And that night there was another meeting of the gang in the bedroom.

"We'll dispense with the Minutes of the last Meeting," Richard began formally, then opened his mind to all of them. Up until then the gang had been acting on orders, although from the things they had been doing they must have guessed what he intended, but now they *knew*. He gave them all the pieces of the puzzle and showed them how it fitted together.

The evasions of their parents, the overflowing toy stores and the computers which could direct a rocket to any spot in the world. A strangely uncomfortable deputy Santa—they must have had some kind of hold over him at the store—and secret caverns guarded by angry soldiers and storekeepers who were robbers. And juvenile delinquents, and a Santa Claus who couldn't be found because he must have run away and hidden himself because he was ashamed to face the children and tell them that all their toys had been stolen.

Obviously the juvenile delinquents had raided Santa's toy caverns and cleaned them out, leaving only big people's toys which the adults themselves no longer wanted—this explained why Santa's guards were so mad at everybody. Then the stolen toys had been sent to the storekeepers, who were probably in cahoots with the delinquents. It was as simple as that. Santa just would not be coming around this Christmas and nobody would get any toys, unless the gang did something about it . . .

". . . We're going to see that the children get *some-*

thing," Richard went on grimly. "But none of us is going to get what he asked for. There is no way of telling which one of all those hundreds of rockets is meant for any one of us. So we'll just have to take what comes. The only good thing is that we're going to make Christmas come three days early.

"All right, gang, let's get started."

Buster returned to the room where he had been given candy the night before, the room with the man who watched a screen with a white line going round on it. But he stayed hidden this time—he was merely acting as the gang's eyes. Then Mub and Loo, linked to the distant room through Buster's and Richard's minds, began to move the grown-up who sat before the screen. More precisely, they moved his hand and arm in the direction of the big red button.

But the grown-up didn't want to push the button and make blips. He struggled to pull back his hand so hard that Loo complained that it was hurting her head. Then they all got together—Liam, Greg, Buster and the girls—and concentrated. The man's finger started moving toward the button again and he began to shout to somebody on the radio. Then he drew his gun with the other hand and hit his arm with it, knocking it away from the button. He was being very, very naughty.

"Why don't we push the button," Greg asked suddenly, "instead of making the grown-up push it?"

Richard felt his face going red, *he* should have thought of that. Within a second the big red button drove down into the bottom of its socket.

The Early Warning systems were efficient on both sides. Within three minutes all forty-seven missile bases had launched or were launching their rockets. It was an automatic process, there were no last-minute checks, the missiles being maintained in constant readiness. In those same three minutes orders went out to missile-carrying submarines to take up previously assigned positions off enemy coasts, and giant bombers screamed away from airfields which expected total annihilation before the last one was off. Like two vast, opposing shoals of fish the missiles slid spaceward, their numbers thinned—but only slightly—by the suicidal frenzy of the anti-missiles. The shoals dispersed and curved groundward again, dead on course, to strike dead on target. The casualty and damage reports began coming in.

Seventeen people injured by falling plaster or masonry; impact craters twenty feet across in the middle of city streets; tens of thousands of dollars and pounds and rubles worth of damage. It was not long before urgent messages were going out to recall the subs and bombers. Before anything else was tried the authorities had to know why every missile that had been sent against the enemy, and every missile that the enemy had sent against them, had failed to explode.

They also wanted to know who or what had been making rocket base personnel on both sides do and see things which they didn't want to. And why an examination of the dud missiles revealed the shattered and fused remains of train sets and toy six-shooters, and if this could have any possible connection with the robberies of large toy stores in such widely separate places as Salt Lake City, Irkutsk, Londonderry and Tokyo. Tentatively at first both sides came together to compare notes, their intense curiosity to know what the blazes had *happened* being one thing they had in common. Later, of course, they discovered other things...

That year Christmas came with the beginnings of a lasting peace on Earth, although six members of a young and very talented gang did not appreciate this. The toys which they had put in the noses of the rockets to replace the sparkly stuff—which they had dumped in the ocean because the grown-ups didn't want it— had failed to reach them. They had been worrying in case they had done something very wrong or been very bad. They couldn't have been *very* bad, however, because Santa came just as they had been told he would, on a sleigh with reindeer.

They were asleep at the time, though, and didn't see it.

ARTHUR C. CLARKE'S VENUS PRIME™

by Paul Preuss

VOLUME 1: BREAKING STRAIN   75344-8/$3.95 US/$4.95 CAN
Her code name is Sparta. Her beauty veils a mysterious past and
abilities of superhuman dimension, the product of advanced
biotechnology.

VOLUME 2: MAELSTROM   75345-6/$3.95 US/$4.95 CAN
When a team of scientists is trapped in the gaseous inferno of
Venus, Sparta must risk her life to save them.

VOLUME 3: HIDE AND SEEK   75346-4/$3.95 US/$4.95 CAN
When the theft of an alien artifact, evidence of extraterrestrial
life, leads to two murders, Sparta must risk her life and identity
to solve the case.

VOLUME 4: THE MEDUSA ENCOUNTER
75348-0/$3.95 US/$4.95 CAN
Sparta's recovery from her last mission is interrupted as she sets
out on an interplanetary investigation of her host, the Space
Board.

VOLUME 5: THE DIAMOND MOON
75349-9/$3.95 US/$4.95 CAN
Sparta's mission is to monitor the exploration of Jupiter's moon,
Amalthea, by the renowned Professor J.Q.R. Forester.

Each volume features a special technical infopak,
including blueprints of the structures of *Venus Prime*

THE CONTINUATION
OF THE FABULOUS
INCARNATIONS OF IMMORTALITY
SERIES

PIERS ANTHONY

FOR LOVE OF EVIL
75285-9/$4.95 US/$5.95 Can

Coming Soon
from Avon Books

AND ETERNITY
75286-7